Alabama
State Facts

Nickname:	Heart of Dixie/Cotton State
Date Entered Union:	December 14, 1819 (the 22nd state)
Motto:	*Audemus jura nostra defendere* (We dare defend our rights)
Alabama Men:	Hank Aaron, *baseball player* Nat "King" Cole, *entertainer* Joe Louis, *boxer* Lionel Hampton, *jazz musician*
Flower:	Camellia
Bird:	Yellowhammer
Fun Fact:	The music group Alabama has a fan club and museum in Fort Payne

Rhys Wakefield had been hiding one great-looking body!

That was Angie's first thought as she entered her boss's bedroom and saw him propped up in bed, feverish but gorgeous, the sheet riding low on his hips. "How do you feel?"

"Lousy," he growled impatiently. "Where's the file I asked you to bring?"

"On your desk at the office," Angie replied, calmly shaking down the thermometer she'd found at his bedside.

Rhys closed his mouth by instinct when she pushed the thermometer into it. Glaring at her, he removed it.

Angie leaned closer, her face only inches from his. "If you don't keep that thermometer in your mouth, I'm going to be forced to take your temperature in a considerably less dignified manner...."

"Don't make threats unless you're fully prepared to carry them out, *Angelique*," he said in a soft, intimate tone.

"I never do," she whispered, forgetting the thermometer, forgetting everything. "I never do...."

American
HEROES
AGAINST ALL ODDS

GINA
WILKINS
After Hours

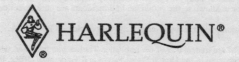

HARLEQUIN®

TORONTO • NEW YORK • LONDON
AMSTERDAM • PARIS • SYDNEY • HAMBURG
STOCKHOLM • ATHENS • TOKYO • MILAN • MADRID
PRAGUE • WARSAW • BUDAPEST • AUCKLAND

For Mamaw

HARLEQUIN BOOKS
225 Duncan Mill Road, Don Mills,
Ontario, Canada M3B 3K9

ISBN 0-373-82199-9

AFTER HOURS

Copyright © 1990 by Gina Wilkins

This edition published by arrangement with Harlequin Books S.A.

® and TM are trademarks of the publisher. Trademarks indicated with
® are registered in the United States Patent and Trademark Office, the
Canadian Trade Marks Office and in other countries.

Visit us at www.eHarlequin.com

Printed in U.S.A.

About the Author

Bestselling and award-winning author **Gina Wilkins** has written more than fifty books for Harlequin and Silhouette Books. Her novels are sold in more than one hundred countries and are translated into twenty languages.

Books by Gina Wilkins

Harlequin Temptation

Hero in Disguise #174
Hero for the Asking #198
Hero by Nature #204
Cause for Celebration #212
A Bright Idea #245
A Stroke of Genius #262
Could It Be Magic #283
Changing the Rules #299
After Hours #309
A Rebel at Heart #337
A Perfect Stranger #353
Hotline #369
Taking a Chance on Love #392
Designs on Love #400
At Long Last Love #408
When It's Right #454
Rafe's Island #458
As Luck Would Have It #470
Just Her Luck #486
Gold and Glitter #501
Undercover Baby #521
I Won't! #539
All I Want for Christmas #567
A Wish for Love #592
A Night To Remember #620
The Getaway Bride #633
Seducing Savannah #668
Tempting Tara #676
Enticing Emily #684
The Rebel's Return #710
It Takes a Hero #729
The Littlest Stowaway #749

Silhouette Special Edition

The Father Next Door #1082
It Could Happen to You #1119
Valentine Baby #1153
†*Her Very Own Family* #1243
†*That First Special Kiss* #1269

†Family Found: Sons & Daughters

Previously published as Gina Ferris

Silhouette Special Edition

Healing Sympathy #496
Lady Beware #549
In from the Rain #677
Prodigal Father #711
*Full of Grace #793
*Hardworking Man #806
*Fair and Wise #819
*Far To Go #862
**Loving and Giving* #879
Babies on Board #913

*Family Found

Previously published as Gina Ferris Wilkins

Silhouette Special Edition

‡*A Man for Mom* #955
‡*A Match for Celia* #967
‡*A Home for Adam* #980
‡*Cody's Fiancée* #1006

‡The Family Way

Silhouette Books

Mother's Day Collection 1995
Three Mothers and a Cradle
"Beginnings"

Dear Reader,

I wrote *After Hours* after reading about a family who had lost everything in a fire. Though all of their belongings were gone, the family insisted that they were fortunate because their only real treasures—their loved ones—had survived. The article made me think about how we often believe that our belongings are what make a home. When Angelique St. Clair loses all her possessions in a fire, she learns the truth of the old saying "Home is where the heart is." I hope you enjoy this story of two wounded people who learn what a treasure true love can be.

Warmest regards,

Gina Wilkins

Please address questions and book requests to:
Harlequin Reader Service
U.S.: 3010 Walden Ave., P.O. Box 1325, Buffalo, NY 14269
Canadian: P.O. Box 609, Fort Erie, Ont. L2A 5X3

1

"...AND IN ADDITION, I would certainly have quite a few suggestions to make concerning your distribution system. I've had several courses in computer distribution, with state-of-the-art training in the field of..."

Nodding rather grimly, Rhys Wakefield made a nominal show of interest in the eager young applicant's babble, but the truth was, he'd made up his mind almost the moment the expensively suited young woman had entered the room. *No.* No to this one, no to the earnest young man with horn-rimmed glasses and a five-hundred-dollar briefcase who'd preceded her, no to the man before him and the woman before him. Bunch of smug, overly confident college graduates who thought that four to six years of classroom lectures and a framed document declaring them well educated made them experts in the world of business. The world Rhys had entered at the bottom and conquered through backbreaking effort, inhuman hours and sheer, single-minded determination.

He'd hocked himself to his earlobes to purchase a struggling little industrial equipment manufacturing plant, renamed it WakeTech Industries and turned it into a Fortune 500 company within ten years. It was his company, his life, and damned if he was going to let some wet-behind-the-ears college kid come in as his executive assistant only to start telling him how to improve his operation. All of the applicants so far had begun the interviews by telling him the wonderful plans they had for the company, as if hoping to impress him with their bright ideas. What the hell made them think he wanted their advice?

He wanted—no, he needed—an assistant, not a partner. He'd envisioned someone loyal, eager, dedicated—and, yes, humbly subservient. Though intelligence was a must, formal education wasn't important, and neither were gender, race, sexual orientation or religious preference. So why hadn't he found anyone who'd even come close?

He could only be grateful that he hadn't given in to his personnel administrator's urgings to allow her to do her job and hire his assistant for him. Heaven only knows which of the smart-aleck whiz kids he'd have ended up with. He'd continue to do without until he found someone who fit the image he preferred.

Taking advantage of the woman's pause to draw breath, Rhys broke in firmly. "Thank you, Ms.—" he had to stop to look down at her application, having forgotten her name "—Baker, but I'm afraid you're not right for this position. However, I will send your application to the personnel office to be kept on file in case a suitable position does come open." The words came out in a weary monotone, having been said so many times before that he now recited them by rote.

Looking slightly incredulous, Ms. Baker tried once more to assure him that he really couldn't continue to do business without her. Rhys had the distinct impression that she left him with the belief that the prosperous company would be bankrupt within days because he'd held firm to his decision not to hire her.

Alone in his office once more, he ran a hand over his

roughly hewn face in a tired, discouraged gesture and groaned. There was still one applicant left to interview that afternoon. Lord, he hated this. Why on earth had he allowed himself to be talked into hiring an assistant?

He reached for his phone. "Send in the last one, June," he ordered with a curtness due—this time—to frustration and boredom. June complied with his instructions without protest, having grown accustomed to her employer's gruff, no-nonsense manner in the six years she'd worked as his secretary.

Rhys opened the last application on the desk in front of him, not bothering to lift his eyes from it as someone entered his office. Angelique St. Clair, according to the neatly filled-out form. "Sit down, Ms. St. Clair," he instructed without polite preliminaries.

Peripherally aware that his directive had been obeyed, he scanned the application, his eyebrows lifting in proportion to his growing interest. As far as he could tell from reading the terse answers to the standard questions, this person was totally unqualified for the position as it had been advertised. A twenty-six-year-old liberal arts graduate from an expensive Eastern college who claimed to have experience as a social secretary to an unnamed financier, Angelique St. Clair had given no references, listed no boastful accomplishments. Rhys was definitely intrigued.

He lifted narrowed gray eyes to examine the young woman sitting absolutely still in the deep leather chair before his massive desk.

She was much too pretty, was his first thought. His second was that she looked even younger than her application claimed her to be. Could be a problem. A delicate blonde may have a tendency to burst into tears the first time he snarled at her. And he would snarl. He'd never claimed to be the easiest guy in the world to work for.

And then he studied the wide-set, clear violet eyes meeting his steadily, bravely, and he noted the not very well concealed glint that could indicate a stubborn streak. Perhaps a bit of temper. Neither of those possibilities concerned him. He had enough obstinacy and more than enough temper of his own to outmatch even the foolhardiest opponent, never mind a young, fresh-faced blonde who'd probably come only to his chin. And he'd never cared for weaklings, despite his insistence on absolute compliance from his employees.

"Tell me why I should hire you as my assistant, Ms. St. Clair," he began bluntly, his eyes never leaving her face.

Angie took a deep breath, determined not to show this man how nervous he was making her. She'd expected someone older and, she'd hoped, a bit less intimidating. When she'd first seen him, his silver head bent over her application, she'd thought her prior estimate of his age had been correct. And then he'd looked up and she'd realized her error.

Prematurely gray, Rhys Wakefield was probably not a day over forty. A hard, lean, somewhat weathered forty, but still a good fifteen years younger than she'd expected from his reputation. One tough son of a gun, she'd been told. A hard-nosed businessman with a ruthless drive to be the top in his field, a workaholic who seemed to have few of the needs mere mortals require—food, sleep, entertainment, that sort of thing. A man who controlled his many well-paid, multi-benefited employees with no more than an expressive lift of his straight dark brows. Her tentative inquiries had netted that much, but no one had mentioned that Rhys was relatively young, roughly handsome and as fascinating as he was terrifying.

His voice was deep, clipped, slightly rough edged. She could detect no particular accent, which sounded rather odd to her after four weeks in Birmingham, surrounded by the slow, soft drawl of the Deep South. Something told her that Wakefield would have no patience for prevarication, no tolerance for bluff. His narrowed gray eyes would spot a lie before it even left her mouth. Tilting her chin, she decided to lay all her cards in front of him. She'd never really expected to get this job, anyway. But, perhaps, if she impressed him enough, he'd find a place for her somewhere in his organization.

"I realize that I have no formal training or experience as an executive assistant to the CEO of a company such as WakeTech," she admitted levelly. "But I can assure you, Mr. Wakefield, that should you hire me, I would be the most dedicated, loyal, hardworking employee on your staff. I learn quickly, I take instructions well, I know when to keep my mouth shut, and I have no aspirations to power or fancy titles. I need a job. I would do nothing that would put me in danger of losing it."

Damn, Rhys thought, holding his expression carefully impassive. This one definitely had possibilities, despite her fragile appearance and slightly uppity Boston accent. "You've given no references and precious little history on your application, Ms. St. Clair. Mind if I ask why?"

This was it. Her refusal to give references and her reticence about her past had lost her every other job she'd applied for since arriving in Birmingham a

month earlier. Resisting the urge to cross her fingers—
or to beg—she continued to meet those piercing dark
eyes with her own and answered clearly. "I have no
references, Mr. Wakefield, and my past has no rele-
vance to my performance as your employee."

Rhys eyed her in silence for a long, taut moment,
then closed her file. "I'm not an easy boss, Ms. St. Clair.
I'm fair, but demanding. I pay well, but you work hard
for every penny you earn. The hours will be long and
strenuous, the days off will be rare. I don't give flowery
compliments for work well-done, but I don't hesitate to
point out errors. I don't like training new people, so I
want you to decide now whether you're going to up
and quit when the going gets too tough."

"I'm not a quitter, Mr. Wakefield. And, as I said, I
need this job." She tried not to let her rush of optimism
show in her expression.

"Then be here in the morning at eight. And get a
good night's sleep. You're going to need it."

She didn't even smile. "Yes, sir. Will there be anything else, Mr. Wakefield?"

"That's all. Stop by personnel on your way out and
you'll be given insurance forms and anything else they
need you to fill out. Oh, and Ms. St. Clair—"

She was already up from her chair. She paused.
"Yes, sir?"

He smiled. "Welcome to WakeTech."

"Thank you, Mr. Wakefield. You won't regret hiring
me." She turned and left his office, golden head high,
slender shoulders squared, the straight skirt to her sen-
sible gray suit swaying softly around perfectly formed
legs that looked impossibly long for her no more than
five-feet-five-inch height.

Watching those legs until the door closed behind

her, Rhys resisted the urge to clear his throat. "I hope not," he muttered in response to her parting words. "I sincerely hope not, Ms. St. Clair."

"HOW DID IT GO?" Rhys's secretary, June Hailey, inquired as Angie passed her desk.

Here was the Southern accent Angie had expected— warm, friendly, unabashedly curious. "I got the job," she confided, unable to quite hide her exuberance for the moment. Almost immediately after the smile spread across her face, she suppressed it, replacing it with a more professional, more distant expression. She had no interest in making friends with June or anyone else in her new firm, though she hoped to maintain a pleasant working relationship with all her co-workers. Her life was in chaos, her self-respect in shreds. It would be a long time before she trusted anyone enough to let them get close to her again. All she needed now was her job, her privacy and the refuge of the small, comfortably furnished house her grandmother had left her. Maybe there would come a day when she'd need more. But she had a lot to prove to herself before then.

Accepting June's warm congratulations with a rather brusque nod, Angie headed for the personnel office with long, confident strides. And tried to convince herself that Rhys Wakefield's smile hadn't just turned her inside out.

RHYS WAS QUITE PLEASED with his new assistant over the next few weeks. He'd subtly tested her mettle almost immediately after she'd begun working for him when she'd misspelled his name on a report—she'd made the common error of spelling it phonetically,

Reese. He'd corrected her rather too bluntly, but other than looking a bit embarrassed at her gaffe, she'd handled the criticism very well. She worked hard, she learned quickly, she didn't fall apart when he yelled at her, and she kept her opinions to herself unless he asked for them. And she was very nice to look at, a fact that was occasionally as uncomfortable as it was pleasant.

He noticed her appearance all too often, his attention caught by a toss of her golden hair, a shrug of her slender shoulders, the gleam of indirect lighting on her long, smooth crossed legs as she took notes he dictated to her. He found himself remembering those images during odd times when he was alone—in his office in the evenings, at home on those rare occasions when he wasn't at the office. He'd had beautiful women working for him before, but there had never been one to interest him quite as much as Angelique St. Clair.

He couldn't help wondering about her. Her rare smiles were distant, polite, very professional. He'd never heard her laugh. If she'd made any friends in the company, he wasn't aware of it. She never protested his requests that she work late or arrive early or come in on weekends during particularly busy times, so if there was a lover, he wasn't a demanding one. For some reason, Rhys suspected that there was no lover. And yet he'd developed some pretty good instincts about people over the years. There was much more to Angelique St. Clair than she allowed anyone to see. Humor, temper, passion—he believed those emotions simmered beneath the lid she'd clamped so firmly upon them. When and why had she decided to adopt such a cool, aloof faȧde? What was a woman who'd obviously grown up in the upper echelons of Boston society doing in Birmingham, Alabama, working as his assistant?

He told himself he had no business wondering. Her privacy was to be respected, as was his. He too kept himself at a distance from others, for what he considered to be very good reasons. He should be relieved, actually. He'd had a secretary once who'd made the silly mistake of believing herself in love with him. It had gotten very awkward, very messy before he'd finally been forced to discharge her in a scene he still couldn't remember without wincing. Thank goodness there'd be no risk of anything like that happening with Ms. St. Clair. She was too good an assistant to lose over something so unreasonable.

So, he'd stop wondering what it would be like to stroke those long, silky legs. Stop wondering how those soft, slightly pouty lips would taste. Stop imagining that slender, nicely curved body beneath his. Shifting uncomfortably in his desk chair, he scowled down at the readout in front of him, realizing he'd completely lost his concentration. Damn. Maybe it had been too long since he'd been with a woman. Too bad there wasn't a conveniently uncomplicated one around who interested him even a fraction as much as his puzzling assistant.

SPINNING HER CHAIR to face the window of her office, Angie hung up the telephone with a grimace she would not have indulged had anyone been in the room with her. She'd just completed a call to an associate in California, and the man had made every effort to be the breezy L.A. cliché. Weariness making her a bit giddy, in addition to missing both breakfast and lunch that day, she lifted her nose in a mock-snooty expression.

"Fan-*tas*-tic, sweetheart. It's a done deal," she mimicked wickedly. "Have your people do lunch with my people. Ciao." And then she laughed softly at her own foolishness.

"Let me guess. You've been talking to Henderson in L.A.," drawled a deep voice from the doorway behind her.

Angie closed her eyes in a mortified wince. Of all people to catch her indulging in a rare bit of frivolity, it would have to be Mr. Wakefield! Composing her expression, she turned her chair around. "Yes, I was," she admitted, glancing up at him. Something in his gray eyes caught her attention for a moment. A gleam of shared amusement? A momentary awareness of her as a person, not simply an employee? Surely not, she told herself, dropping her eyes back to her desk. "I have the figures here you requested, Mr. Wakefield. As you can see, they're almost exactly as you'd predicted."

She handed him the report she'd just finished, noting when she did so that his eyes had returned to normal. Shuttered, inscrutable. And she chided herself sternly for unreasonably feeling a bit disappointed that the brief moment of communication was over.

For the remainder of the day, she was especially careful to be even more efficient and professional than usual. If her employer noted any difference in her behavior, he didn't comment. But then, he never did.

SITTING ALONE IN A BOOTH in a trendy restaurant close to her office, Angie scanned *The Wall Street Journal* as she finished her salad. Having lunch was a rare luxury for her. Rhys—as she called him only in her mind these days—usually kept her so busy there wasn't time for such leisure. His two-day business trip to Dallas was giving her a break, of sorts—one of the few in the four months she'd worked for him. Not that she'd slacked off at the office, of course. But without Rhys's constant instructions, she was able to do her work *and* have time for lunch. As hard as she'd worked during the past months, she still didn't have the same stamina her employer displayed. *She* sometimes needed to rest. He apparently did not.

A familiar voice from the other side of the stained-glass divider that separated her booth from the adjoining one caught her attention. Darla, one of the secretaries from the office, spoke quite clearly. "Did you hear that the new engineer made a pass at the deputy dictator today?"

The answering laugh was also known to her—Gay Webster, from data processing. "Poor man. Was he still in one piece when she finished with him?"

"Mmm. I hear he hasn't stopped shaking yet, though. And his color may never be the same. Seems he's a bit pale."

"Frostbite, most likely. How anyone that gorgeous on the outside could be so cold and hard on the inside is totally beyond me."

"You want to know something really funny? When Mr. Wakefield first hired her, I thought maybe she was his mistress. It wouldn't be the first time a man hired his girlfriend for a highly paid assistant's position. I must have been temporarily delusional. I mean, we both know neither Wakefield nor St. Clair have the same urges as most other humans. They're as cold to each other as they are to everyone else. Shoot, they probably don't even *have* sex. With anyone."

Gay laughed again. "Ain't it the truth. But if there

was ever a perfect pair, those two would be it. Both of them hard as nails, perfectionists, real loners. It's not as if either of them are overtly unfriendly to any of us. They're polite enough, unless someone steps out of line, of course. But—brr! Cold is the right description."

Perhaps a third of her salad still lay on her plate, but Angie had suddenly lost her appetite. Pushing the plate away, she picked up her purse, carefully folded her newspaper and stood. Her movement drew the attention of the two women in the next booth. Angie noted that both of her co-workers looked immediately horrified to recognize her. She nodded coolly to them. "Hello, Gay. Darla. Enjoying your lunch?"

She didn't wait for them to answer, but walked away with her chin high, her pace unhurried. She found some comfort in the knowledge that no observer could have possibly known how deeply she'd just been hurt.

Hard as nails. Loner. Cold. And they'd been talking about her. Echoes of voices from the past filled her mind as she drove mechanically back to the office.

Hey, Party Angel! Give us one of your beautiful smiles.

Oh, Angie, you're such a cutup. Aren't you ever serious?

We're bored, Angie. Do one of your funny monologues. Make us laugh.

Gosh, I envy you, Angie. You're beautiful and rich and popular. You're so lucky, Angie.

So lucky. Angie nearly gave into an unladylike snort as she shoved the gearshift of the aging sedan into park after maneuvering it into her private parking space in the WakeTech lot. How things changed. How *she* had changed.

As she turned the key in the door of the battered ten-year-old car, she thought fleetingly of a candy-apple-red sportscar. Yes, things had definitely changed.

SHE TRIED VERY HARD not to dwell on her co-workers' spiteful words as she worked that afternoon. Afternoon stretched into early evening and still she sat, shuffling papers, studying numbers, perusing correspondence. She would not leave until everything was ready for Rhys's return the next morning.

Rhys. *If there was ever a perfect pair, those two would be it.* Gay's words slammed into her mind with an almost physical punch. Angie had been so very careful not to even mentally acknowledge her nagging attraction to her employer during the past months. It hadn't always been easy. More than once a meeting of eyes, an accidental touch, a very brief moment of shared amusement had weakened her resistance, made her tremble with a wholly unwanted awareness of Rhys Wakefield, the man. Yet she'd managed to maintain an emotional distance at all times. She hadn't recovered enough from past wounds to allow herself to form even the beginnings of a relationship. She had no intention of becoming involved with her complex, brilliant, unfathomable employer.

Not that she had anything to fear on that score, she thought soberly. There had been times when she'd wondered if Rhys even noticed that she was a woman—not that she would have it any other way, of course. It was simply that she was accustomed to being pampered and admired, both for her looks and for her former wealth and social position. Her illogical feminine ego had taken some comfort from the passes she'd intercepted initially from various male co-workers, though after several months of icily determined refusals, even the most ardent pursuer had conceded defeat. Only the occasional newcomer dared make advances to her now. And that was exactly the way she wanted it.

Though her own reasons for solitude were simple enough, she couldn't help wondering why an attractive, seemingly healthy male such as Rhys would be rumored to live an almost monklike existence. He was always the first to arrive and the last to leave the office, weekdays, weekends and holidays. If he were seeing anyone, Angie couldn't imagine when he would find the time.

She slammed a folder closed with more force than necessary. Rhys Wakefield's social life was none of her business, she reminded herself sternly. She had work to do, and plenty of problems of her own to occupy her thoughts.

Work completed, she reached for her purse in preparation to leave. Feeling a bit disheveled, she pulled out a small mirror to check her discreet makeup and neatly pinned hair. Something about the unsmiling, sensibly attired image in the mirror held her still for a long time. When the reflected woman's full lower lip quivered, she didn't even notice a film of unexpected, unwelcome tears suddenly obscuring her vision. Shoving the mirror into her purse, she rested her forehead on her hand, swallowing an inexplicable sob.

RHYS STOOD IN THE OPEN DOORWAY, frowning at the sad-looking figure behind the desk. She hadn't heard him open the door, and he wondered fleetingly if he could step out and close it again with equal unobtrusiveness. For the first time in the four months that he'd worked with her, Angelique St. Clair looked vulnerable, even a bit lost. And for the first time in his entire life, Rhys Wakefield found himself fighting the urge to take a woman in his arms and simply hold her, murmuring words of comfort.

That atypical impulse was extraordinary enough to make him frown in bewilderment. *What* words of comfort? Even if he was foolish enough to give in to the urge, he wouldn't know what to say. And she'd probably think he'd lost his mind. She wasn't the type of woman who'd appreciate a man's shoulder to cry into. She'd rather take care of her own problems. Wouldn't she?

He cleared his throat.

Angie jumped and whipped her head around, her hand going to her mouth. She dropped it immediately. "Oh, I—you startled me," she said rather breathlessly, unnecessarily. She schooled her expression to the calm, impassive one she always wore, only a trace of sadness lingering in her violet eyes. "I wasn't expecting you to come in until tomorrow."

"I wanted to pick up a few things on the way home from the airport," he replied, then asked awkwardly, "Is there—uh—is anything wrong, Ms. St. Clair?"

Her smile was bright and blatantly insecure. "Of course not, Mr. Wakefield. Was there something you needed?"

"The Garver file. Do you have it?"

"Yes, sir. Here it is. Is there anything else?"

Taking the file, he continued to study her. Her chin lifted and she met his eyes steadily, no expression showing on her pale, composed face. "No, that's all," he said after a moment. "It's getting late. Why don't you go on home."

"I was just getting ready to leave," she agreed, standing, purse in hand. "Good night, Mr. Wakefield. I'll see you in the morning."

"Good night, Ms. St. Clair. Sleep well," he bade her impulsively.

If the uncharacteristic send-off startled her, she didn't show it. "Thank you, Mr. Wakefield. I intend to."

Sometime in the early hours of morning, Rhys found himself hoping she *was* sleeping well. Damned if he was. Lying in his bed, staring at the ceiling—a familiar position to a chronic insomniac such as Rhys—he couldn't erase the image of her sitting so small and forlorn in the large office chair, her slender shoulders bowed under a massive imaginary weight. What was haunting Angelique St. Clair? What in her past had been so traumatic that it had turned a beautiful, naturally warm-natured young woman into a reclusive, work-obsessed automaton?

Would he ever find out? And did he really want to? Or was he correct in his suspicion that getting too close to his beautiful blond assistant could disrupt his entire life?

2

IT WAS A SATURDAY in early May, beautiful, warm, fragrant. Angie had the day off. What luxury!

She did her weekly cleaning that morning, carefully dusting the furnishings and knickknacks that were still arranged exactly as they had been when Grandma Neal had died nearly a year earlier. Angie's happiest memories of childhood were of the rare visits she'd been allowed with her maternal grandparents, who'd had little extra money but had always been rich in love. The house they'd left her was small, had a few maintenance problems, was far from luxurious, but Angie was content here, particularly now that she was beginning to build a small savings account from the salary she was earning at WakeTech.

She'd spent her first month in Birmingham desperately looking for a job, watching helplessly as the few dollars she'd been left after her father's trial had rapidly dwindled. Her first paychecks had gone for payments on overdue bills and for clothing suitable to her position, replacing the glittering gowns and designer suits and sports clothes left behind in Boston. She took great pride in her new wardrobe. Though not as stylish or expensive, these garments were bought for herself, by herself, purchased with clean, honestly earned money.

Her father's profitable shady business dealings had

kept her in the lap of luxury, but she felt no gratitude to him now. He was serving time in a country-club prison, the shallow, materialistic crowd she'd once called her friends had long since deserted her, and Angie was completely alone. She'd suffered the mortification of being investigated, suspected of being a knowing accomplice in her father's crooked deals simply because she'd worked as his social secretary for five years after graduating college.

She winced. Social secretary. He'd called her that as justification for the extravagant salary he'd paid her. Actually, she'd done very little other than to keep his calendar straight and serve as hostess for the many functions he deemed necessary for persons of their social standing.

Everything they'd owned had been sold to pay fines and the taxes Nolan had so skillfully avoided over the years. All those things she'd purchased with her "salary," all those expensive gifts he had lavished on her. All gone. But she was making it, dammit, despite her father's frequently expressed doubts that she would manage to get by on her own, without guidance from him or one of the upwardly mobile, morally deficient young men he'd urged her to wed. *So, there, Dad.*

Something inside her softened when she dusted a silver-framed portrait of her grandparents that had been kept on the piecrust occasional table for as long as Angie could remember. They would have believed in her, she mused, studying the strong-charactered faces depicted in the photograph. Though her grandfather had died many years ago, she remembered him as a hardworking, unassuming, honest man who quoted the Bible and Aesop with equal fervor. Never at a loss for an encouraging platitude.

Her grandmother, whom Angie had frankly adored, had been kind, loving and cheerful, though she'd never gotten over her disappointment that Angie's mother had placed luxury above sentiment. Margaret had been a beautiful, rather spoiled young woman who'd headed East in search of stardom and ended up married to an ambitious, cunningly intelligent man who'd promised her everything and then proceeded to give it to her, regardless of how he obtained it.

Angie had often wondered if, prior to her death ten years earlier, Margaret had been more aware than her daughter that Nolan's business dealings had occasionally strayed to the wrong side of the law. Angie felt guilty that she'd been so smugly complacent with her self-indulgent life-style that she'd been blind to harsh reality until her father's arrest. Still grieving over her grandmother's death a month prior to the arrest, Angie had taken a long look at her life during those stressful months of her father's trial—and what she had seen had sickened her. So here she was, trying to make something of herself, trying to prove that she was more than a spoiled, decorative socialite.

"I wish you were here, Grandma," she murmured to the sweetly lined face in the photograph. "I miss you."

Sometimes the loneliness was overwhelming. But how could she make friends before she proved herself worthy of friendship—*real* friendship? Not the shallow games played by her set in Boston, the falsely amiable competition to be the most chic, the most visible, the most outrageous. Angie wasn't even sure she knew how to be a friend, much less offer anything more lasting—such as love.

The chime of her doorbell made her replace the photograph with a curious frown. She couldn't imagine who would be visiting her. Even after five months in Birmingham, there was no one she knew well enough to expect them to drop in unannounced. Crossing the room to answer the door, she wondered why she suddenly thought of Rhys. And she wondered why she was suddenly having trouble breathing.

She told herself that she was *not* disappointed to find a small freckled-face boy of about seven on the doorstep, a tiny black-and-white kitten in his rather grubby arms. She recognized the child as a neighbor she'd seen playing on the sidewalks in this quiet middle-class neighborhood. "May I help you?"

The boy grinned winningly, displaying several gaps where teeth should be. "My cat had kittens and my mom said I had to give them away. This is the last one. Would you take her, ma'am?"

"Oh, I—"

"She's a good kitten, ma'am," the boy assured her earnestly, blue eyes almost round with youthful sincerity. "She don't need to go outside if you've got a litter box and she'll be good company. She's had her shots and she's real healthy. And she won't cost you nothing—well, except for food and litter. Course, she's a girl, so she'll have to have an operation. My cat's getting an operation tomorrow. That way she won't have no more kittens. My mom said that was the only way we could keep her."

Good company. The two words seemed to leap out of the breathless monologue. Angie eyed the mewing kitten. "Well..."

Sensing victory, the boy looked even more sweetly innocent and held the cat out to Angie. "You want to hold her? She's real soft."

Angie had her hands full of kitten almost before she

realized it. Nuzzling the warm little body against her cheek, she smiled at the contented rumble that emanated from the kitten's chest. "What's her name?"

"She don't have one yet. You can name her whatever you want. But I like 'Flower.'"

"Flower?" Angie looked at the child with a lifted eyebrow.

"Sure, cause she's black-and-white like a skunk. Don't you remember *Bambi*?" he asked when Angie still didn't respond. "Bambi thinks the skunk is a flower, so he calls it 'Flower.'"

It made sense, in a weird sort of way. "Flower," Angie repeated thoughtfully. Dumb name for a cat. But, then, she'd never expected to be the owner of a cat. "What's *your* name?" she asked the boy.

"Mickey."

"Well, Mickey, thank you for the kitten. I'll take very good care of her. And you can come visit her anytime you like," she added impetuously.

Mickey's round face lit up with an ear-to-ear grin. "Gee, thanks, ma'am. My mom will be real happy with me for finding homes for all four kittens in one day. I gotta go. Bye."

Angie closed the door and looked down in bemusement at her new pet. Her first friend, she thought with a whimsical smile. And then she carried Flower into the bedroom with her, to keep her company while she changed. It seemed she had some kitty supplies to buy.

ANGIE STOWED HER BAG in her desk early Monday morning, then smiled as she brushed a few cat hairs from her dark skirt. She'd felt a bit guilty leaving Flower alone that morning, though she'd made sure litter box, food and water, soft bed and favorite toys were

all accessible. It was rather nice to know there would
be someone waiting to welcome her when she got
home that evening.

Perhaps it was that warm thought that made her
look up with a smile when someone tapped tentatively
on the open door to her office. Her smile dimmed
when she noted Darla and Gay standing in the doorway, both young women looking decidedly nervous.
Gay, the pretty redhead from the computer department, spoke first, "May we have a word with you, Ms.
St. Clair?"

Wishing she could refuse, Angie nodded. "Yes, of
course. Come in."

Darla, the slightly overweight brunette secretary, entered first, with Gay close behind. She took a deep
breath, expanding her generous bosom impressively.
"Ms. St. Clair, Gay and I feel awful about what you
overheard at lunch Friday. What we said was completely out of line and we're very sorry."

Angie nodded without expression. "Consider it forgotten."

Gay shook her head. "That's not enough. We know
we hurt you. And we feel terrible about it."

"You didn't—" Angie began automatically, and
then stopped. "Yes, you did hurt me," she acknowl-
edged after a pause. "But you were only saying what
you really thought."

Darla chewed her lip guiltily, her big brown eyes
visibly sympathetic at Angie's uncharacteristic admission of having feelings. "It's just that we haven't had a
chance to get to know you, Ms. St. Clair. What we said
was inexcusable, but we—well, we were just cutting
up. Being silly—you know."

Of course she knew. How many times had Angie

and her country club "friends" engaged in wicked lunchtime humor at the expense of others? "I understand. Please don't worry anymore about it."

Gay spoke again. "We're going to try the new Italian place down the street for lunch today. Would you like to join us, Ms. St. Clair?"

Her first impulse was to politely decline. Her second was a more honest one. She wanted to accept, dammit. She was tired of eating alone, being alone all the time. If Rhys protested her taking the hour off, she'd tell him that she deserved a lunch hour, just like everyone else. "I'd like that. Thank you for asking me. And, please, call me Angie."

The two women looked slightly dazed at her acceptance, but both hastily assured her they would be delighted to have her join them. Telling her they'd meet her downstairs at noon, they returned to their work, leaving Angie with a rather bewildered smile. It had taken a lot of courage for them to approach her that way, she mused, thinking of the vicious gossip she'd overheard more than once after her father's arrest. None of the so-called friends she'd caught in their whispers had ever apologized—or tried to make amends by asking her to have lunch with them. Her father's tainted name had made her less than a desirable member of the privileged circle.

She suspected that the two young working-class women who'd just left her office had more character and depth than any of the jet-setters she'd socialized with in her past. She couldn't help wondering if they'd be as willing to accept her as a friend if they knew about her father.

ANGIE WAS INTERRUPTED again by a voice from her doorway late one Friday morning, nearly a month after

Darla and Gay had made their first overture. "Excuse me, Ms. St. Clair."

Angie looked up from her overflowing desk. "Yes, June?"

Rhys's secretary, her hands full of papers, winced her apology at disturbing Angie's work. "I'm sorry to bother you, but you wouldn't happen to know where Mr. Wakefield is, would you? It's after eleven and I haven't heard from him today. Maybe he told me he wasn't coming in this morning, but if he did, I forgot."

Angie frowned. She'd wondered why Rhys hadn't called for her his usual dozen times that morning; she'd assumed he'd been unusually busy. "He didn't come in this morning?"

"No. And I don't know what to do with these papers. They need his signature."

"But he said yesterday that he'd be here first thing to work on the London deal. I've been expecting him to call me in all morning."

June shrugged. "I don't know what to say. He's never done this before, not in the entire six years I've worked for him."

Angie had worked for him for only five months, but she was as well aware as June that it wasn't like Rhys to simply not show up for work, without at least a telephone call. A dozen possible reasons flashed through her mind, and none of them were pleasant ones. Her stomach tightening, she reached for her phone and dialed his home number.

Listening to the ringing on the other end, she told herself she was overreacting. She was going to feel really stupid if some breathless woman answered, if it turned out that her employer was simply taking the morning off for a bit of prurient pleasure. And then she told herself that the thought greatly disturbed her only because she had too much respect for Rhys as a businessman to believe he'd be so irresponsible.

When the phone rang for the fifth time without answer, she began to worry again. What if he couldn't answer? What if he were hurt or—

"What is it?"

The hoarse growl made her shoulders relax in relief. "Thank goodness," she said without thinking.

There was a pause and then, "Ms. St. Clair? What time is— Oh, hell." His voice was decidedly raw.

"Are you ill, Mr. Wakefield?" Angie asked in concern.

He coughed roughly. "Yeah, I guess I am," he grated, sounding rather surprised that he was susceptible to the same weaknesses as everyone else. "Damn."

"Were you sleeping?"

"Yeah. I couldn't sleep last night and I must have—" He broke off for another spell of coughing, followed by an impatient expletive.

Fighting a smile now, as well as an utterly incomprehensible surge of tenderness at the image of her intimidating employer in bed, tousled and heavy eyed and flushed with fever, Angie clutched the receiver more tightly. "What can I do to help?" she asked simply.

The sound of movement came through the line. "Nothing," Rhys muttered. "I'll be there in—" His voice broke off as something crashed. "Damn."

"Mr. Wakefield? What's wrong?"

"Dizzy," he answered curtly.

"Then lie back down. And don't even think of coming to the office today. Who's your doctor?"

"I don't need a doctor. And I have to come in. Those papers on the London deal have to be signed today. And I—"

"I'll bring the papers to you," Angie interrupted firmly. "And anything else that must have your attention today. The other matters can wait until you're feeling better."

He sighed. "All right," he conceded reluctantly. "Bring them to me. Get the spare key from June and just come on in. And while you're at it, get the Perkins file. And the..."

Scribbling the list of items he deemed in need of immediate attention, Angie made a rash decision to omit several of them. He'd snarl, but it wouldn't be the first time. The man was ill. The company wasn't going to fold if he gave himself a day or two to recuperate. "I'll be there in half an hour," she promised.

"Fifteen minutes," he argued, just before she hung up on him.

She looked at June, who still hovered nearby. "Mr. Wakefield is ill. I'm to bring him some things he needs to work at home today."

"Mr. Wakefield is ill?" June repeated. "What's wrong with him?"

"It sounded as if he has a bad cold—maybe flu."

A low chuckle escaped the ever-efficient secretary. "Bet the boss hates that," she commented, setting the stack of papers on Angie's desk. "Bested by a common cold. Who'd have believed a cold germ would have had the courage to take him on?"

Angie couldn't help laughing. June eyed her with surprised pleasure. Flushing a bit, Angie dropped her eyes and began to gather a few things to take to Rhys. "Thank you, June. That will be all."

"Yes, Ms. St. Clair," June replied immediately, but there was a new note of friendliness in her voice this time that Angie didn't miss.

She sighed when she was alone once again. She really wasn't doing a very good job of staying aloof and distant. Even though that first luncheon had been a bit awkward as Angie had tried to make conversation without revealing too much about herself, Gay and Darla had invited her twice more to eat with them. She'd had to decline both times because Rhys had kept her too busy to do more than grab a sandwich at the snack bar downstairs, but they'd seemed inclined to invite her again and always made a point to speak to her when they passed in the hall.

Mickey stopped by her house on occasional afternoons on the pretense of visiting her rapidly growing kitten, but mostly because she'd started keeping cookies in the house for him. And she was having a particularly hard time maintaining a safe distance from her attractive boss, though she still wasn't particularly popular among the other men at WakeTech. Why was it that when she'd wanted friends, none had been available for her, and now that she wanted to be alone, she was beginning to get close to people?

Shaking her head at the complexities of her life, she headed for Rhys's office to gather the papers he'd requested.

HER LEFT ARM LOADED with the things—well, most of the things—Rhys had requested from the office, Angie paused before inserting the key June had given her into the lock of his front door. It was the first time she'd seen his house, a large, though rather plain contemporary home in an exclusive neighborhood not far from the more modest subdivision in which Angie lived. There was something a bit too intimate about just opening the door and walking in, though she didn't want to disturb him by ringing the doorbell. Taking a deep breath, she turned the knob.

Rhys was obviously into minimalism in his decor, was her first observation when she stepped inside the house. Though what was there was top quality, the furnishings were plain, functional and included only essential pieces. A few paintings hung on the walls, but had not been placed with regard to balance or style. There were no knickknacks, photographs or other personal memorabilia.

She thought of a Boston mansion decorated by the trendiest designers, colors and accoutrements changed for each season. Original old masters' paintings, sterling silver paperweights, crystal chandeliers. Her childhood bedroom, with its yards of antique lace and shelves of Madame Alexander dolls.

She thought of her grandmother's house, with its profusion of porcelain figurines, candy dishes and doilies. The chipped ceramic dog in the foyer, the mismatched plates in the antique china cabinet, the dimestore print of the *Last Supper* hanging in the dining room. The patchwork quilts and crocheted afghans her grandmother had made. The crayon drawings Angie had mailed her over the years, all carefully preserved and kept in a scrapbook on the old upright piano, along with numerous photographs of Angie at various stages of growing up. And she wouldn't have traded her current home for the most elegant, high-priced house in Birmingham—or anywhere else, for that matter.

Glancing around uncertainly, she headed for the

stairway, assuming Rhys's bedroom was upstairs. Rhys's bedroom. She swallowed nervously.

The first door on the right at the top of the stairs was open. Peeking inside, she realized she'd found the master bedroom. The only furnishings were a bed and a large dresser, a nightstand containing a lamp, an alarm clock and a telephone, and a straight-backed chair over which was draped the jacket to the suit Rhys had worn to the office the day before. One painting hung on the wall above the bed—a rather lonely looking scene of a storm-swept seascape. Rhys sprawled in the bed, sound asleep.

Tiptoeing across the plush cream-colored carpet, she paused by the side of the bed, gazing down at her employer. He looked very much as she'd pictured him— tousled, fever flushed, unshaven. Though she'd been prepared to see him that way, the reality still took her aback. He looked so very different from the arrogant, unapproachable man she'd worked with for the past five months. He looked sick and alone. She knew he'd violently reject her sympathy, but it went out to him anyway.

Frowning at the color in his flat, lean cheeks, she wondered how high his fever was and whether he'd taken anything for it. She reached toward him, snatched her hand back, then slowly reached out again, compelled by her concern for him. He was sleeping so soundly. Maybe she wouldn't disturb him if she—

Her hand had hardly touched his skin before her wrist was caught in a painful iron-hard grip. "Ouch!"

Still holding her wrist, her palm trapped against his temple, Rhys stared up at her, his dark gray eyes a bit bleary but as piercing as ever. "What are you doing?"

"You looked feverish," she replied as evenly as possible under the circumstances. "And your face feels very hot. Have you taken your temperature?"

"No."

"Have you taken any medication for it? Aspirin?"

"No."

"Would you mind letting go of my hand?" she asked carefully. "You're bruising my wrist."

He released her immediately. "Sorry. I'm not used to being touched while I'm sleeping."

"Then I'm sorry I startled you. How do you feel?"

"Lousy," he growled, looking impatient.

She held on to her own patience with an effort. "Is your throat sore? Does your head hurt? Is there any other pain?"

"My throat's sore, my head hurts and I ache all over. Is that what you want to hear?" he snapped, propping himself up on one elbow. The sheet that had been draped over him when she'd entered fell to his waist. Angie very nearly dropped her armload of papers.

Rhys Wakefield had been hiding one great-looking body beneath those severely tailored dark business suits.

His chest was broad, tanned and solid, sculpted with the firm muscles of a natural athlete. In contrast to his thick silver mane, the hair on his chest was dark, sparse, angling down from his nipples to a thin line that disappeared beneath the sheet. She couldn't help mentally following that line further down, which made her knees go weak.

"You—uh—" She stopped, cleared her throat and lifted her eyes back to his face, intercepting an odd, fleeting expression that he repressed immediately.

"You'd better lie back down. Do you have a thermometer?"

"In the bathroom. But—"

She didn't give him time to argue. Laying the reports on the foot of the bed, she turned and hurried into the adjoining bath, needing a few moments alone to regain her composure.

Rhys was coughing when she returned, a thermometer, a bottle of aspirin and her self-control all firmly in hand. The cough was deep and sounded terribly uncomfortable, though he appeared to be more concerned with looking through the papers she'd brought him. "Where's the Perkins file?" he demanded when he'd caught his breath.

"On your desk at the office," Angie replied, calmly shaking down the thermometer. "There's nothing in it that needs your attention before Monday, at the earliest."

"Dammit, I—mmph." He closed his mouth by instinct when she pushed the thermometer into it. Glaring at her, he removed it. "You didn't bring the report on the San Juan deal, either."

"No, I didn't. That's been taken care of." She took the thermometer from his hand and replaced it in his mouth.

He pulled it out again. "Taken care of by whom?"

"By me. And if you don't keep that thermometer in your mouth, I'm going to be forced to take your temperature in a considerably less dignified manner," she threatened, frustration temporarily overcoming the composed discretion she'd so carefully cultivated during the past months as his assistant. She'd sounded very much like the old Angie just then, she realized

with a mental wince, waiting fatalistically for Rhys to
fire her on the spot.

She was surprised when he did nothing more than
stare at her hard for a long, taut moment and then
slowly place the thermometer back in his mouth. She
had enough sense not to express satisfaction that he'd
followed her order.

"I'll get you something cold to drink," she muttered,
avoiding his eyes as she turned to leave the room.
"You're supposed to drink plenty of liquids when you
have the flu."

Rhys's kitchen had the look of a room that was
equipped strictly for convenience, used no more than
absolutely necessary. His refrigerator contained
canned soft drinks—he seemed to have an unexpected
taste for fruit-flavored sodas such as orange, grape and
strawberry—a jug of orange juice, a gallon of milk, a
half-dozen eggs, butter and blackberry jam. That was
it. She poured him a large glass of orange juice, deciding she'd ask if he was hungry before trying to make
breakfast from his limited supplies.

The thermometer was still in his mouth, apparently
forgotten, when she walked back into his bedroom.
Rhys was absorbed in the material she'd brought from
the office. She set the juice on the nightstand and
reached for the thermometer. "I need a pen," he announced the moment his mouth was free.

"Just a moment," she replied absently, squinting at
the tiny numbers on the side of the thermometer and
wishing he had one of the newer, digital models. Finally lining up the mercury, she frowned as she read
the temperature. "Your temperature is one hundred
and three degrees."

He barely flicked her a glance. "I'll take some aspirin. Where's that pen?"

She sighed, handed him two aspirin and the juice and rummaged in her purse for a pen. "Are you sure you don't want me to call your doctor?" she asked, handing it to him.

His answer was a grunt. She assumed it was a negative one. "Then how about something to eat? I could make you an egg and some toast."

"Not hungry." He coughed again.

"Do you have any cough medicine?"

"No."

"I'll go the nearest pharmacy and get you some. Your chest will get sore if you keep coughing that hard. Do you need anything else while I'm out?"

"The Perkins file," he answered promptly.

She picked up her purse and turned without responding to that. "I'll be back soon."

He caught her wrist before she could step away, surprising her into immobility. His skin burned against hers, and she had to remind herself that it was only because of his fever. She looked up to find him smiling very faintly at her, causing another jolt of awareness to ripple through her. "Thanks," he said quietly.

She managed not to gulp. "You're welcome, Mr. Wakefield." She added the formal address deliberately, to remind herself—and possibly him—that their relationship was strictly a professional one.

He released her and she moved toward the doorway. She paused again when he spoke her name. "Ms. St. Clair."

"Yes, sir?"

The smile was gone, though his gray eyes held a gleam that was hard to interpret. "A word of advice.

Never make threats unless you're fully prepared to carry them out."

She'd wondered whether he'd mention her threat with the thermometer. She intended only to nod and walk away, but her tongue was being very recalcitrant that day. "I never do, Mr. Wakefield," she said with cool precision.

And then she made her escape, amazed at her own temerity.

3

RETURNING FROM her quick shopping trip, Angie placed the grocery items in the kitchen, found a spoon and headed back upstairs with the cough medicine the pharmacist had recommended. Her eyes on the empty bed, she stopped in the doorway to Rhys's room. Where was he?

A cough from the door to the bathroom drew her attention there. Wearing nothing but a pair of white briefs, Rhys stood braced with one arm against the doorjamb, looking at the bed as if there were an arduous obstacle course between it and him. Angie had already seen his chest and arms, but now she was able to examine the rest of him. Powerful legs lightly covered with dark hair, lean hips, flat stomach. The white briefs stood out in glaring relief against his tanned skin, clinging revealingly to the quite impressive rest of him. She found herself incongruously wondering how old he was, if her guess of forty was even close. Though his hair was silver and his eyes and mouth bracketed by fine, deep lines, he had the body of a man ten years younger than her estimate.

And then he looked up and caught her staring at him.

Her cheeks going pink, Angie started to back out of the room. "Excuse me, I—"

"I don't think I can make it to the bed," he interrupted quietly, his frustration with the admission evident in the hard set of his jaw. "My knees feel like they're going to give out on me."

Forgetting her embarrassment, Angie rushed to his side. "Lean on me, then. You shouldn't have gotten up."

"I didn't have a hell of a lot of choice," he growled wryly, though he draped his arm around her shoulders cooperatively enough.

Angie told herself that her knees trembled only because he was leaning so heavily against her and not because his long, lean, nearly naked body was pressed so closely to hers, letting her feel the heat and strength of him even through her prim dove-gray business suit. She couldn't remember the last time any man had affected her quite this way—or had there ever been another time? She hadn't come even this close to intimacy with a man in a very long time. Unlike most of her former set, Angie had never cared for casual bedhopping, never indulged in the one-night stands discussed so coyly, so avidly over lunch at the club. Angie had always wanted to care, but the caring had always led to disappointment.

She couldn't allow herself to start caring now. Most of all, not with this man, who would be so unlikely to offer anything in return.

"When's the last time you had anything to eat?" she asked, determinedly channeling her thoughts to a more practical topic.

He shrugged as he sank gratefully back onto the bed. "I wasn't hungry last night."

"And lunch yesterday was a sandwich at your desk." She shook her head. "No wonder you're weak.

Between the fever and lack of food, I'm surprised you didn't pass out at my feet."

"Used to having men at your feet, are you, Boston?"

The drawled question took her aback. She frowned down at him, noting the faintest teasing twinkle in his usually unreadable eyes. He'd never teased her before. And he'd never called her anything but that stiff, formal "Ms. St. Clair." Granted, it was rather hard to be formal when he was wearing nothing but a much-too-thin layer of white cotton knit that covered only the essentials of modesty. Still, she wasn't quite ready for a more personal relationship with him than the one they'd had for the past five months. Deciding to ignore his question—and hoping he'd take the hint—she stepped back. "I bought some soup while I was out. I'll heat it up. Are you sure you won't let me call your doctor?"

He gave her a look she knew well enough to recognize as a signal for her to drop the subject. Resisting the urge to sigh again, she started grimly back to the kitchen.

Waiting on her sick, nearly naked employer was definitely not in her job description, she told herself as she prepared the soup. She really should take him a tray and then get herself back to the office.

Even as the thought crossed her mind, she knew she wouldn't be able to leave him as long as he seemed to need her. It was a unique feeling. No one had ever really needed her before. She decided that was part of the reason she liked her job so much. Rhys obviously needed help at the office and she'd been able to provide that help. And now he needed her again. No, she couldn't just walk away.

RHYS WAS LYING VERY STILL, his eyes closed, when Angie carried the tray into the bedroom. She paused, thinking that if he was asleep, she wouldn't wake him. But then his lashes lifted heavily. With visible effort, he pushed himself upright, the sheet draped once again over his lap. Angie tried not to show her relief that he was at least partially covered, nor her concern with his condition.

"I'm assuming you'll want to feed yourself," she remarked brightly, setting the tray carefully on his thighs.

"You assume correctly, Ms. St. Clair."

So he *had* gotten the message that she didn't want him reading too much into her taking care of him. Good. After all, she was only being a dedicated employee, right? Her gaze drifted across his chest as she stepped away from the bed. Sure she was.

"Call the office. Tell June to call Phelps and cancel our meeting for this afternoon. And tell her to messenger the Perkins file to me. You can take these papers back when you go and fax them to London."

"Yes, Mr. Wakefield. Eat your soup."

His impatient exhale was robbed of its effectiveness by the coughing spell that followed. Angie held the tray steady until he'd stopped coughing, taking care that the hot soup did not splash onto his lap. "I forgot to give you the cough medicine earlier," she commented, hoping he wouldn't realize that the sight of him in his underwear had driven the medicine completely from her mind. She reached for it and poured a dose into the spoon she'd brought.

Rhys's eyes met hers as she spooned the elixir into his mouth. Her hand was trembling when she pulled it back. Damn him for doing that to her. And damn her for being weak enough to let him.

"I'll go wash this spoon," she said rather breathlessly, backing away.

"Do it later," Rhys ordered irritably. "You've bounced in and out of here for the past hour. Sit down."

Biting her lip at his tone, she obeyed, carefully avoiding wrinkling his suit jacket as she perched on the edge of the chair.

Rhys almost sighed. Dammit, now she looked as if she expected him to throw something at her. She'd been as nervous as a cat since she'd arrived, despite that brief show of bravado over the thermometer. He realized the circumstances were a bit awkward, but they'd been working together for five months, spending more hours together than some married couples. She'd seemed comfortable enough with him in the past. Why was she looking at him now as if he were some kind of ax murderer?

"Why don't you remove the jacket so you can get comfortable," he suggested, trying to make his tone more conciliatory. "We need to discuss some things before you go back to the office."

She nodded and stood again, carefully hanging the jacket in the closet before returning to the chair and reaching for a steno pad and the pen he'd used to sign the London papers. She sat with the pen poised, ready to begin, still looking decidedly wary. He noted that she was taking great care not to look at his chest, and he remembered the expression on her face when she'd seen him standing in the doorway in his underwear. Surely she'd seen a man in his briefs before—and less. She was young, but not *that* young.

This time Rhys did sigh. "Would you relax? I know I'm not in the greatest mood, but I'm not going to physically attack you."

Angie's cheeks went pink. The blush was rather charming, but Rhys tried hard to ignore it as she spoke quickly. "Yes, sir. I'm sorry, sir. It's just—"

"And stop calling me 'sir' with every breath!" he interrupted curtly, annoyance growing.

Biting her lip, Angie glanced down at her lap.

Resisting an inexplicable impulse to apologize, Rhys scowled and turned his attention to his soup. "It's good," he said after a few unenthusiastic bites.

Taking the compliment as an apology, of sorts—which, of course, Rhys had meant for it to be—she spoke lightly. "Thanks, but it doesn't take a lot of cooking talent to open a can. Hardly the kind of soup your mother probably made when you were sick as a child."

Rhys's mouth quirked at that. "The only thing my mother ever made for me, as far as I remember, was a note she pinned to my shirt, giving my first name and my date of birth." And then he almost bit his tongue. What in hell had made him tell her that? It wasn't exactly something he went around telling people.

Angie's expression was a mixture of horror and sympathy, neither of which he found particularly gratifying. "You were abandoned?"

Concentrating on his soup, he nodded. "Yeah. Left in the lobby of a hospital in Texas."

"How old were you?"

"Three."

"How terrible. Did you—were you adopted?" Angie asked carefully.

"No. People wanted babies. And I never was a cute, cuddly child, even then."

He could feel her eyes on him as he finished the soup, knew she was trying not to ask more questions, sensed the exact moment her curiosity got the better of her. "Were you raised in an orphanage?"

He lifted one shoulder in a shrug of sorts. "Sometimes. Sometimes foster homes. I hung in until I graduated from high school, then ended up drafted before summer was over."

"You were in the war?"

"Mmm." He swallowed the last of the soup as he mumbled an affirmative.

"You said only your first name was given?"

"Yeah. I didn't know my real last name. Wakefield was a social worker's idea."

"The spelling of your first name is unusual," she commented, still very carefully.

"Welsh," he agreed. "Could've been a traditional name in my mother's family. Who knows?"

"You've never tried to find out more about her?"

"No." He shoved the tray to the foot of the bed, tired of that subject. He couldn't read the expression in Angie's deep violet eyes, nor did he want to try at the moment. "Want to get back to work now or would you rather swap life stories?"

He was well aware of her reaction to the rather sarcastic suggestion. It was as if she'd made a physical retreat, drawing back into herself before he caught a glimpse of something she didn't want him to see. He couldn't help but wonder what she was trying to hide. Not that it mattered. She was a good assistant. As far as he was concerned, her past had nothing to do with her job for him. As for his personal curiosity—well, that was something he'd have to ignore.

Setting the tray aside, he sank down onto the pillows, silently cursing his aching head and overall weakness, and began to spout instructions in a terse, rapid tone. He told himself he wanted to hurry her on her way to get everything done that required her attention, that he needed to sleep and didn't want her hovering over him as he did so. And yet he was aware of an odd reluctance for her to leave, a feeling of emptiness at the thought of being alone and feeling so rotten.

Must be the fever making him light-headed, he decided, grimly turning his thoughts to work.

HALF AN HOUR LATER, Angie closed the steno pad and stood, reaching for her purse. She had to get back to the office if she was going to finish everything he wanted done before the end of the working day. Rhys lay wearily against the pillows, eyelids drooping, face pale except for the two spots of color on his cheeks indicating his fever hadn't completely receded. The medicine had helped some, but the racking cough still escaped him occasionally, making his chest contract so sharply her own ached in empathy. She took the tray to the kitchen, rinsed the soup dish, then filled another glass with orange juice.

"You'd better take a couple more aspirin," she suggested when she carried the juice into the bedroom. "You need to try to keep that fever down."

He took the aspirin without protest, his uncharacteristic docility making her worry even more. "Isn't there someone I can call to stay with you awhile?" she asked. "I hate leaving you alone." She knew now that there was no family, but surely a friend? A—it was hard to even form the word in her mind, for some reason—a lover?

His eyes closed, Rhys shook his head against the pillows, his silver hair ruffling appealingly. "I'll be okay. You'd better go on. Don't forget to call Ron Anderson."

"I won't. I'll check on you later. Call the office if you need anything, all right?"

"Mmm." He cracked one eye to look up at her. "Thanks again. For everything."

"You're welcome, Mr. Wakefield."

He was scowling when he closed his eye again. She wasn't quite sure what she'd said to displease him. He was asleep even as she left the room, casting one last glance back from the doorway and feeling strangely guilty as she turned and walked away.

BY LATE AFTERNOON, Angie realized that she hadn't had a bite to eat all day. Deciding to take an afternoon break, she shoved some money into the pocket of her suit jacket and walked to the company snack bar, where a number of her associates had gathered for a coffee break. She noted the curiosity on several faces at her almost unprecedented appearance during this scheduled leisure time. Ignoring them, she bought an apple and a soft drink from the vending machines lined along one wall and turned to find a table.

Gay's voice caught her attention. "Angie. Over here."

Gay and Darla were sitting at a long, rectangular table with several other women, all of whom were looking at Gay in surprise at her show of friendliness to Mr. Wakefield's habitually aloof assistant. A bit defiantly, Angie took the one empty chair at the table, giving Gay and Darla a bright smile. "Hi."

The others blinked as if they were astonished that Angie even knew how to smile. For the first time Angie wondered if maybe she'd gone overboard in keeping to herself until she'd sorted out her personal problems. Had she really been so intimidatingly unapproachable? She hadn't even known she was capable of intimidating people. She'd never had problems making friends before—though now she knew how much money and social position had impressed those so-called friends.

"June told us Mr. Wakefield is ill," Darla said sympathetically. "Do you know what's wrong with him?"

"Flu, I think. He has a fever and a bad cough and he says his throat's sore and he aches all over."

"You went to see him, didn't you?" Gay asked, eyeing Angie curiously.

"I took some papers for his signature."

Leaning her chin on one hand, Gay smiled. "I'll bet Mr. Wakefield's a lousy patient."

Angie couldn't hold back a chuckle. "You'd win the bet. He is."

One of the other women, an attractive blonde whose name Angie didn't know, shuddered dramatically. "I'd be terrified to actually go into his home when he was ill and in a bad mood. He scares me enough when I pass him in the hall here at work."

"He's not really so scary," Angie felt compelled to say. "He's just—well, he's a classic workaholic. He gets wrapped up in his responsibilities and forgets about the social niceties." Even as the words left her mouth, she flushed, realizing how neatly she'd summed up her own behavior of the past few months. She decided right then to make a point to be more friendly to her co-workers in the future. Starting immediately.

SHE WORKED UNTIL after six that evening. Heading wearily for her car, she wrestled with an unwelcome urge to drive straight to Rhys's house to check on him. He hadn't asked her to come back, she reminded herself practically. She had no intention of taking any more work to him, hoping he'd give himself the weekend at least to recuperate. He was perfectly capable of calling someone if he needed anything.

Sighing deeply, she slammed the car door shut and shoved her key into the ignition. Of course she was going to his house. She simply couldn't rest easily that evening until she'd made certain that he was all right.

Ridiculous, of course, to worry about a tough, fiercely self-sufficient man such as Rhys Wakefield. But he seemed so very much alone. Being in a similar situation herself, she could imagine how miserable she'd be if she was to come down with his flu. Maybe he wouldn't appreciate her concern, but she seemed to have no choice. She still hadn't gotten over the aching sympathy she'd felt upon hearing that he'd been abandoned, raised without a home or family. Her own mother was dead and her father had proven that he couldn't be trusted, but at least they'd seen that Angie had had a reasonably happy childhood. Poor Rhys.

Poor Rhys? She snorted at the fleeting thought, knowing how he'd repudiate her pity. She turned the key, then groaned aloud when the engine made a strange grinding sound. "Not again," she muttered in disgust. The aging car needed more maintenance than she could afford to pay just then. Probably more than it was worth, actually. She'd love to trade, but was still reluctant to take on an additional payment until her finances were more secure. If the car would last only another three or four months, maybe then she'd be more comfortable about trading.

"Come on, start," she urged, pumping the gas. She

exhaled in relief when the engine caught, though it sounded rough. At least it was running.

She hesitated at Rhys's front door. Should she use the key again? Would he consider that too presumptuous since she was stopping by on her own initiative this time and not at his request? She should have called from the office, she decided belatedly.

Perhaps she should ring the bell. Her finger hovered over the button as a new worry plagued her. What if he was still dizzy? Picturing the stairs to his bedroom, she winced at the thought of him tumbling down them.

She couldn't risk that, she decided, fitting the key to the lock. She'd apologize for barging in and explain her reservations about ringing the bell. He might not appreciate her consideration, but at least he'd know her reasoning.

Impulsively she stopped by the kitchen, pouring another large glass of juice. Walking quietly up the stairs with the glass, she paused at his open doorway. He was lying on his back in the bed, his right arm covering his eyes, his left hand moving restlessly on his chest as if to massage an ache. A muffled groan drew her inside the room. "Mr. Wakefield?" she said softly, trying not to startle him. "Are you feeling worse?"

He lowered his arm slowly, looking over it with red-rimmed eyes. "What are you doing back? Did something happen at the office? What went wrong?"

"Nothing went wrong," she assured him, stopping beside his bed and setting the juice on the now-crowded nightstand. "I just wanted to stop by on my way home to check on you. How do you feel?"

His answer succinctly summed up his condition. Accustomed to his blunt speaking after five months of working at his side, Angie only nodded. "I thought so. Have you checked your temperature lately?"

She could tell by his expression that he had not. Shaking her head, she popped the thermometer into his mouth. He cooperated, but his expression told her he was thinking of that other time, as she was. Though she'd assured the young secretary that Rhys wasn't such a scary person, she wondered now how she'd ever found the nerve to actually threaten him.

Angie bit her lip as she read the thermometer. The mercury rested steadily between one hundred three and one hundred four degrees. "It's not going down. Have you been taking aspirin?"

His frown told her that he hadn't taken anything since she'd left him. "Honestly," she scolded, reaching for the aspirin bottle sitting on his nightstand. "If you still refuse to see a doctor, the least you can do is take care of yourself. Do you want to end up in a hospital?"

She gave him two aspirin, then handed him the juice to wash them down. Rhys swallowed the tablets, then shot her an oddly amused look. "Are you fussing over me, Ms. St. Clair?"

"I suppose I am," she admitted. "Do you mind?"

"Not at the moment."

She smiled at that. "I'll try not to make it a habit."

If she hadn't known better, she'd have thought he seemed a bit disappointed. Ridiculous, of course. Must be a trick of the light.

Rhys took another sip of the orange juice, then jiggled the glass. "There's vodka downstairs. Why don't you bring up a bottle. Strictly for medicinal purposes, of course. You could fix yourself one—call it preventative medicine."

"You don't need it with the cough medicine you're taking and I don't drink," she answered firmly.

His brow quirked curiously. "Never?"

"Never."

"Any particular reason?"

She grimaced. "Yes. An unpleasant experience. I went to a sorority party in my sophomore year in college, drank entirely too much and spent the rest of the year wondering if I'd done anything completely foolish that evening. I have a low tolerance for alcohol. I don't remember a thing after about my third drink until the next morning when I woke up praying to be allowed to die."

"Wake up in a strange bed, Boston?" Rhys asked casually, a hint of a smile playing around his hard mouth.

"I was spared that, thank goodness," she answered fervently. "My roommate took pity on me and hauled me home sometime in the early hours. She told me later that I'd had plenty of offers of other beds to stay in and that I had cheerfully accepted all of them."

"A friendly drunk, are you?"

"Evidently," she agreed. She couldn't quite believe she was chatting with him this way. It was just that he seemed so different away from the office, still flushed with fever, his hair ruffled boyishly over his forehead. So approachable. So—well, so likable.

"So you haven't had a drink since?"

She shook her head firmly. "Not a drop. I never want to lose time like that again. I like to be in control of my actions."

"And a bit more selective about your bedmates?"

She fought down a flush and answered his lazily drawled question in much the same tone. "Exactly. I prefer to be admired for my mind. I don't want to be every guy's idea of an easy blonde."

His gray eyes flicked to her hair. "'Only God, my dear, could love you for yourself alone and not your yellow hair,'" he murmured, his smile deepening just enough to carve a long, straight line into his right cheek. Almost a dimple, she thought wonderingly.

And then she realized what he'd said. "Yeats?" she asked incredulously. "Mr. Wakefield, you read Yeats?"

"I have been known to read for pleasure," he answered coolly.

She flushed, afraid that she'd offended him. "Of course you do. I didn't mean—"

"And don't you think it's time you started calling me 'Rhys'? This 'Mr. Wakefield' stuff is getting pretty ridiculous under the circumstances."

That was something else she hadn't expected. Everyone on his staff called him "Mr. Wakefield," at least in front of her. Though she'd thought of him as "Rhys" for the past few months, she wasn't sure she was ready for the more intimate form of address in actuality. Then again, it had been a direct order, more or less. She decided to agree with him, but to make it a point not to call him *anything* unless necessary. "If you'd like." She quickly changed the subject. "Are you hungry? I could make you another bowl of soup."

He frowned and shook his head. "I'm not hungry."

"You really should eat. You need to try to keep up your strength. If you don't want soup, I could make something else."

His frown deepened. "I don't pay you to cook for me."

"I'm aware of that," she replied steadily. "But someone has to when you can't even get out of bed without falling on your face."

He didn't seem to have an answer for that. Taking advantage of the moment of silence, Angie turned and walked out, determined that he would eat before she left for home.

WHY HAD SHE COME BACK? Rhys wondered, climbing carefully back into the bed after another annoyingly shaky trip to the bathroom. Why was his assistant downstairs in his kitchen, making soup for him? They'd worked together for five months, and she'd never shown much interest in him other than as an employer. But today she'd shown more concern for him than anyone had since—when?

Thinking back, he decided the last time anyone had really cared that he'd been sick had been when he was sixteen and living with his last foster mother, Aunt Iris. She'd cared. Still did, for that matter. She was one of the only two people in the world who really gave a damn about him. He warned himself not to start thinking of Angelique St. Clair as a third person who cared about him. She was just an employee, an excellent assistant who allowed her dedication to her job to spill over to keeping her employer healthy. There could be nothing else between himself and his assistant. She was too young, too vulnerable, to get involved with anyone right now. And he—well, he'd never been any good at relationships. He'd long since stopped trying to build them.

He'd never been very good with people. Perhaps it was because he'd been shuffled from place to place so often as a kid. Always rather introverted, wary of becoming too attached to the families he lived with, because he knew his stay would only be temporary, he'd become more and more of a loner as he'd grown up. Vietnam hadn't changed him for the better, though he'd met his only close friend there, Graham Keating.

Rhys knew the people who worked for him thought him cold, unapproachable, intimidating. That image had served him well, on the whole, ensuring their compliance with his instructions. But there were times even he had to admit that he was rather lonely. He'd never encouraged the attention of women he knew would want more than he felt capable of giving, but the type of women he'd limited himself to had never really filled the gap inside him. Never penetrated his shell of isolation.

Hearing Angie coming up the stairs, he gathered his wondering thoughts with a frown. He was getting maudlin, he decided irritably. Must be getting old. Or maybe it was the fever. He looked up as Angie appeared, carefully balancing a tray, her usually smooth brow creased in concentration, her full lips slightly pursed as she eased into the doorway. Her thick golden hair was somewhat disarrayed, her neat little gray suit wrinkled from a hard day's wear. And he was hit by a sudden surge of desire so intense that he was relieved his lower half was covered with a sheet. Which made it difficult to attribute his responses to illness.

Damn. What was this woman doing to him?

ANGIE STAYED UNTIL RHYS had eaten every drop of the soup. Even then she was reluctant to leave. "You'll take your aspirin every four hours to keep the fever down? And the cough medicine. Don't forget that," she fretted.

"I'll be okay," he assured her, sinking deeper into the pillows.

"I've left my number on the nightstand. Promise you'll call me if you need anything. I really won't mind."

"I'll call. Now go home. You need to rest."

He looked genuinely concerned about her. Angie tried not to be touched. "All right, I'm going." Impulsively she reached out to lay her palm on his forehead, relieved that he seemed cooler than he had when she'd arrived. "Your fever seems to have come down, but you should still keep taking the aspirin."

Rhys reached up to take her wrist, trapping her in her position leaning over him. "You're fussing again," he observed quietly, making her suddenly aware that his face was only a matter of inches from hers.

"I—uh—I'm sorry. I—" Her voice trailed off as their eyes locked. She had to be misinterpreting his expression, she told herself frantically. He couldn't seriously be thinking of kissing her. Could he? "I'd better go."

"Yes, you had," he agreed just a shade too adamantly. "Good night."

She tugged her hand from his. "Good night, Mr.—uh, good night. I'll call you tomorrow to check on you, all right?"

He shrugged, his scowl deepening. She knew he was annoyed that she'd so obviously avoided using his name. "As you wish."

Making her escape with as much dignity as she could maintain, Angie knew she had a great deal to occupy her thoughts that evening. She wondered if she'd ever get to sleep.

4

ANGIE PICKED UP her telephone receiver three times Saturday morning before finally getting the nerve to dial Rhys's number. She'd told him she'd call, of course, and she was anxious to know if his condition had worsened, but...

She couldn't stop thinking about that strangely intimate moment when she'd thought he was going to kiss her. And she couldn't shake the nagging curiosity about what it would have been like if he had.

Stop this, Angelique St. Clair, she ordered herself impatiently, defiantly pressing the first button. *This is your employer you're fantasizing about. How terribly unprofessional of you.*

Rhys answered on the third ring. Though still hoarse, he sounded better than he had the day before.

"How are you feeling?"

"Better," he replied, confirming her guess. "Still got this damned cough, but other than that I'm on the mend."

"That's good news," she assured him, wondering why she wasn't more pleased. Had she subconsciously hoped he'd need her again today? If so, why? "You— um—do you need me to come over?" she heard herself offering anyway. "I could make you something to eat, run some errands, whatever you require."

"No," he answered rather curtly, then seemed to feel

the need to soften the rejection with more explanation. "I'm back on my feet now—the dizziness is gone—so I can handle everything. There's no reason for you to be here."

I don't need you anymore, he was saying. Not in his personal life, anyway. Rather let down by the realization that they were back to business as usual, though she should be relieved, Angie twisted the phone cord around her finger. "I'm glad you're feeling better. I'll see you at the office on Monday?"

"Right. Oh, and, by the way—"

"Yes, sir?"

"Thanks for caring, Angelique."

Angie stared at the receiver after Rhys abruptly disconnected the call. No one had *ever* called her "Angelique," and she was stunned by the sound of that name on his lips. She hung up slowly, telling herself she'd be very glad to get back to normal on Monday. Surely they'd return to being Mr. Wakefield and Ms. St. Clair within the sober confines of the office. It would be much better for all concerned when they did. Much safer for her.

SOMETIME DURING THE NIGHT, Angie woke with a moan, finding her hand at the pounding pulse in her throat, the echo of Rhys's voice ringing in her mind. "Angelique," he'd called her in the dream. And then he'd kissed her senseless.

Wincing at the hazy memory of the rest of the dream, she hid her face in the pillow, groaning in embarrassment.

Her attraction to Rhys Wakefield was growing all out of proportion. She had to get it under control before her professional relationship with him was affected. She couldn't get involved with him, she reminded herself. She was still too vulnerable, still hurting.

She didn't want him to find out about her father. She'd be humiliated if he did, if he thought less of her because of her father's lack of ethics. Rhys was scrupulously honest in his own business dealings; he had no time for anyone he couldn't trust to be equally honorable.

Her past relationships, both friendly and intimate, had disappointed her, left her feeling used and empty. Even if Rhys should want a fling with her—and he'd never indicated that he did—she couldn't risk losing her job when it ended, and she was certain it wouldn't last long. He gave no indication of being interested in long-term commitments. And she had nothing to offer if he was.

She had to get this under control. Had to keep her distance from this man who was getting much too close without even trying. She wondered anxiously if it was already too late to back away from him.

RHYS WAS ALREADY at the office when Angie arrived Monday morning. He was pale, slightly hollow eyed and still racked by an occasional cough, but she could tell that he was near full recovery. Her first reaction when he appeared in the door to her office was to flush scarlet. She tried to hide her odd behavior by "accidentally" dropping her pen behind her desk and bending to pick it up, ordering herself to stop behaving so foolishly. He couldn't possibly know what she'd dreamed simply by looking at her.

"What have you done with it?" he demanded as

soon as she'd straightened in her chair, hoping he'd attribute her heightened color to her bending over.

"What have I done with what, Mr. Wakefield?"

He scowled, though she wasn't sure whether it was because of her return to formality or her unsatisfactory response to his question. "The Perkins file, dammit. I tried all day Friday to get you to bring it to me—which you neglected to do—and now I can't find it."

"It's been taken care of, Mr. Wakefield. The papers have been delivered to Mr. Perkins for his signature. They should be back here later this afternoon."

"When was this done?"

"Friday," she admitted. "It really wasn't very complicated and I knew you were anxious to get the deal wrapped up. I—"

"If I had wanted you to take care of it, I would have instructed you to do so, Ms. St. Clair," Rhys interrupted bitingly.

This time there was nothing she could do to hide her flush of embarrassment. "I'm sorry, sir. I just—"

"Please remember in the future that I hired you to serve as my assistant. If I'd wanted someone who'd feel qualified to take charge around here, I'd have picked one of those smart-ass M.B.A.s who applied for this job."

Angie bit her lip. "Yes, sir."

He glared at her a moment longer, then turned on one heel and stalked away.

For the first time since she'd started working for Rhys, Angie found herself close to tears after one of his diatribes. And she'd worried about getting too deeply involved with him, she thought grimly. He'd made it quite clear that there was nothing to fear on that score. If he felt anything at all for her, even the faintest touch of gratitude—it certainly hadn't been evident in the way he'd just talked to her. She was another employee to him, one he wasn't too pleased with at the moment. In her eagerness to be of assistance to him, she'd overstepped the invisible boundaries he'd erected between himself and everyone else.

She wouldn't make that mistake again.

Taking a deep breath, she busied herself with her work. In that area, at least, she knew exactly what needed to be done.

RHYS FELT LIKE A HEEL. It really hadn't been necessary to jump all over her like that, he told himself, staring morosely at the closed door to his office. Indulging in an uncharacteristic bit of self-analysis, he decided that he'd been so cross with Angelique because he'd needed to reassert control in their relationship—their *business* relationship, he added firmly. It made him uncomfortable that she'd seen him at his worst, weak, sick, unable to walk from the bathroom to the bed without her assistance. Not to mention the dream he'd had last night, in which she had played a prominent, decidedly erotic role.

He'd come to work that morning believing he had things nicely under control again, only to have the unnerving sensation of feeling his mind go blank the moment he'd stepped into her office and seen her sitting behind the desk. She'd looked so beautiful, so distant, so damned desirable that his tongue had gone dry.

When struggling for a moment to think of something to say after she'd retrieved the pen she'd dropped in a moment of clumsiness, the only thing that had come to mind had been the Perkins file. And then he'd jumped down her throat simply because she'd been a bit overzealous in helping him out while he'd been ill. She'd been fully qualified to handle the Perkins deal, and he was well aware of it. He'd been a real jerk to climb all over her for trying to help—especially after she'd been so considerate about taking care of him Friday.

Climb all over her. The subconscious phrase repeated itself, bringing an accompanying image that shot a bolt of arousal right through his abdomen. It really had been too long since he'd been with a woman, he decided grimly.

He owed her an apology.

He swallowed hard.

When was the last time he'd apologized to anyone? Thinking back, he decided it must have been some twenty-five years earlier, when he was fifteen and Aunt Iris had caught him helping himself to a few dollars from her purse. She'd given him what for, he thought with a faint smile of remembrance. He'd already loomed a foot taller than the feisty little woman, but she'd figuratively cut him down to his knees with nothing more than her furious words. When she finished, he was engulfed with remorse, standing with chin on his chest, toe scuffing dejectedly against the worn carpet on her living room floor. And he'd apologized.

Well, she'd *made* him apologize, to be precise, he thought wryly, but he'd meant it, all the same. He'd been her devoted friend ever since. She'd been the first person to care enough about him to chew him out like that.

His spirited assistant reminded him quite a bit of his former foster mother. And now he was going to apologize to Angelique. He reached for the phone, then pulled his hand back. He *would* apologize, he assured himself. He just wasn't quite ready yet.

ANGIE PAUSED OUTSIDE the door to Rhys's office, her heart in her throat. If there was any other way to get his signature on the papers in her hand...

But his secretary was out to lunch, and sliding the papers under the door seemed somewhat lacking in professionalism. Maybe he wasn't in his office at the moment. Maybe she could run in, drop them on his desk with a scribbled note of explanation, then have his secretary bring them to her later. Mentally crossing her fingers, she knocked tentatively on the door.

"Come in."

Her shoulders sagged, then straightened determinedly. Okay, so much for the easy way out. She'd get his signature and she wouldn't let on for a minute that his tantrum that morning had bothered her in any way. Business as usual, she reminded herself. Strictly business.

"I need your signature on these papers for the personnel department, Mr. Wakefield," she explained as she stepped into the office, her eyes not quite meeting his.

He nodded silently, holding out his hand. She kept her gaze trained on the precise knot of his tie as she passed the folder to him. She felt him watching her for a moment longer, and then he opened the folder, scanned the neatly typed papers inside and scrawled his name across the bottom of the final page. "Anything else?" he asked, returning the folder to her.

"No, sir. I'll take these on to personnel now." She turned with barely restrained haste, relieved that the matter had been dealt with so easily. Now, if only she could get out of here and...

No such luck.

"Angelique." His voice was deep and the slightest bit rough.

Oh, heavens. Stiffening her knees, she turned reluctantly. "Yes, Mr. Wakefield?"

He took a deep breath. If she hadn't known better, she would have sworn he was nervous. Ridiculous, of course. "About the Perkins deal—"

She managed not to wince. *Not that again.* "Yes, sir?"

"I'm sorry I yelled at you," he said, the words coming out so quickly they ran together. "You were perfectly justified to take care of it as you did. If I'd been here, I'm sure I would have had you handle it, anyway. I was out of line this morning and I apologize."

She felt her eyes widen and made a deliberate effort not to drop the papers clutched so tightly in her suddenly nerveless hands. "Um—that's quite all right, sir—um, Mr. Wakefield."

"Rhys, dammit!" he exploded unexpectedly. "Why the hell can't you call me by my name?"

She jumped. "I'm sorry, I'm just so used to calling you 'Mr. Wakefield.'"

He sighed deeply and ran a hand through his hair, deliberately relaxing his shoulders. "I know. Dammit, Angelique, you've got me apologizing in one breath and yelling at you with the next. What is it with you?"

He really had to stop calling her that, she thought hazily. If he didn't, it was entirely possible that she was going to melt right at his feet. How was it that he could make her name sound more seductive than the flowery endearments other men had used? "Most people call me 'Angie,'" she said, hoping he'd take the hint.

"My name," he reminded her as if she hadn't spoken. He'd gotten up from his seat behind the desk and now loomed less than two feet in front of her. Those dark brows of his formed a deep V between his intense gray eyes as he stared at her. "Say it."

Confused by his sudden insistence on such a relatively trivial issue, her cheeks uncomfortably warm, Angie cleared her throat. "All right, Rhys. But if you don't mind, I'd prefer to use 'Mr. Wakefield' in public. It sounds more professional."

He nodded curtly, satisfaction written clearly on his arrogantly carved face. "Of course. I would prefer that, myself." His point made, he returned to his seat behind the desk. "Was there anything else, Angelique?"

She received his message clearly enough. Rhys wasn't most people. He'd call her whatever he liked. "No, si—um, no, that's all." She wasn't sure how he felt now about "sir."

He gave what could have been a muffled laugh and shook his head. "Get out of here," he growled lightly, reaching for his telephone.

That sometimes irrepressible imp inside her reappeared at his unexpected chuckle. Angie made a production of throwing him a snappy salute. "Yes, sir. Right away, sir." She whirled with military precision and left the office, back straight, head high. The sound that followed her out was definitely a low laugh.

She made it all the way to her own office before her knees buckled. She fell into her chair with little semblance of grace, unconsciously fanning her face with the folder she'd forgotten to deliver to the personnel office.

If he could put her into this shape with a soft laugh,

what *would* it be like if he actually kissed her? She couldn't help wondering.

BY BREAK TIME that afternoon, Angie knew she may as well take a few minutes to have a soft drink with her co-workers. Heaven knows she was getting little enough done that day.

Gay and Darla were sitting at their usual crowded table when Angie entered the breakroom. She carried her diet soft drink over to them, sliding into an empty chair. The others at the table seemed less surprised to see her this time than they had on Friday, even smiled with cautious welcome.

"How's Mr. Wakefield today?" Darla asked curiously. "Is he completely over his flu? No one has seen him come out of his office except briefly this morning."

"He's trying to catch up," Angie explained. She smiled wryly. "One weekend off and you'd think he'd been gone for a month."

"Is he still being a bear from his illness?" asked the blonde who'd expressed such terror of Rhys on Friday. Angie had learned then that her name was Priscilla.

Strict professionalism and her sense of humor warred for a moment, and then Angie chuckled. "Well, let's say he's still intent on having his own way," she answered tactfully, thinking of his insistence that she call him by his first name in private.

"So what else is new?" Gay murmured into her coffee cup.

"Exactly." Angie's smile deepened.

"Do you really like working so closely with him?" Priscilla asked curiously, unable to conceal her horrified fascination.

Angie thought about the question for a moment. *Did*

she like working with Rhys? She wasn't sure she could be completely objective about her answer. This was no longer just a job, and he no longer just an employer. But...

"Yes, I do," she admitted, knowing she was being completely honest. She genuinely liked working with Rhys and, if she was even more candid, she'd admit that she actually liked Rhys. She decided there was no need to carry honesty that far. She knew how quickly office gossip could develop.

One of the women had been on vacation the week before. She'd brought photographs of her children posed in front of the various tourist attractions they had seen on their car trip. Angie was included when the photographs were passed around to be dutifully admired. Making the appropriate noises of appreciation, she realized that she was finally becoming accepted by her co-workers. Though she couldn't help wondering what would be said about her if the truth was known about her father, she was still pleased by the tentative camaraderie that was developing. She found herself hoping it would last. She'd missed having friends, even if her former friends had proven to be such a major disappointment.

ANGIE WASN'T SURPRISED when Rhys worked late that evening, nor when he made it clear that he expected her to stay to help him. Immersed in business, they worked side by side as they had from the beginning. Though Angie found it progressively easier to say his name as the day passed, and Rhys continued to use her full first name the few times he called her anything, there were no more uncomfortably intimate interludes. If it hadn't been for an occasional clash of glances that lingered too long, Angie would have been convinced that everything was the way it had always been between them. Employer and employee. Nothing more.

Finally breaking away, hungry, tired and emotionally drained, Angie climbed behind the wheel of her car only to have the engine utterly refuse to start. Cursing beneath her breath, she turned the key several more times, frantically pumping the gas. The grating, grinding sound slowed to a series of clicks and, finally, to silence.

Angie brought both hands down hard on the steering wheel. "Damn!"

Of all days for this to have happened. As late as it was, everyone else was gone, other than Rhys and a couple of security guards. Asking Rhys for assistance was out of the question. She decided to approach one of the guards.

But the matter was taken out of her hands when she climbed from her car only to turn and find herself face-to-face with Rhys.

"What's the problem?" he asked.

"My car won't start," she answered reluctantly, clutching her purse tightly in front of her. "It's been threatening to do this for several weeks, but this time it's serious, I'm afraid."

"You've known something was wrong with your car and you haven't done anything about it?" Rhys demanded immediately, planting his hands on his hips beneath his spread suit jacket. "What if your car had broken down in a rough neighborhood at this hour? What if you'd been stranded on the highway? That wasn't very smart of you."

Biting her tongue to keep from answering him in the

same tone, Angie only nodded curtly. "I suppose you're right."

He jerked his head toward his car, parked in its usual space not far from the one she'd been assigned. "Come on. I'll take you home. We'll do something about your car tomorrow."

We? She decided to let that slide for the moment. As for his not-so-gracious offer of a lift, she decided to accept that. It was the least he could do after she'd nursed him back to health, she told herself. "Thank you. I'd appreciate it."

Closing the passenger door of his car behind Angie, Rhys rounded the sleek hood and slid behind the wheel. He shoved the key into the ignition, started the engine, then turned his head to ask his passenger where she lived, only to be stopped short when his gaze fell on her breasts. Even through the fabric of her sensibly cut blue dress, the soft mounds were clearly outlined by the shoulder strap of the safety belt she'd fastened.

He cleared his throat and quickly dropped his eyes. No, bad move. Now he found himself staring at her surprisingly long, slender legs, which she'd crossed at the knees, where her full skirt ended. Damn, but she was beautiful.

"Where do you live?" he asked more gruffly than he'd intended, turning his eyes firmly to the front of the car. He hadn't expected the answer she gave. He passed her neighborhood every time he drove to the office or back home. Following her directions, he guided the car to a small frame house less than half a mile off his usual path.

The house surprised him. Aging and visibly in need of a few repairs, it seemed totally out of character for his glamorous assistant with her decidedly upper-class speech and behavior. "Lived here long?" he inquired mildly, stopping in the short driveway.

"Since I moved to Birmingham," she answered. "This was my grandparents' home for many years. My grandmother passed away last year and left me the house."

Rhys noted the pleasure on her face and in her voice as she looked at the timeworn structure. She obviously had some very strong ties to this house. Funny, he hadn't expected that she was the type to be so sentimental. Funny, too, how her fondness for the little house drew him to her all the more.

On an impulse he didn't stop to analyze, he said, "Let's go somewhere for dinner. I'll bring you back after we've eaten."

Angie turned to him in apparent surprise. "Dinner?" she repeated rather blankly.

"Yes, dinner," he repeated, his mouth quirking into a smile. "You know—food?"

He wasn't at all pleased with the look that came into her violet eyes. He would almost call it panic. He knew before she spoke that she was going to refuse. "Thank you for offering," she said with careful courtesy, "but I think I'll pass tonight, if you don't mind. It's been a long day and I'm really tired."

"Too tired to eat?" he questioned lightly, giving it one more try.

"Too tired to eat out," she returned. Her hand was already on the door handle.

Rhys conceded defeat for the moment. He wanted some time to think about the look he'd seen in her eyes and to try to decide what it had meant. Why would

Angelique be afraid of him? "I'll walk you to the door."

"No, thank you," she said much too quickly. "It's really not necessary."

He nodded. "All right. Then I'll see you in the morning—seven forty-five?"

She looked questioningly at him. She always reported to work promptly at eight. "You need me to come in early tomorrow?"

He shook his head patiently. "You have no way to get to the office in the morning, remember? I'll pick you up at seven forty-five."

"Oh, you don't need to do that. I can—"

"I'll pick you up," he repeated firmly. "It's on my way. No trouble at all."

She moistened her lips, and he fought down an almost overwhelming urge to kiss her until she was forced to acknowledge that the awareness growing stronger all the time between them was not entirely one-sided. He took some satisfaction in knowing that she couldn't possibly read the impulse in his expression.

Finally she nodded and gave him a rather weak smile. "All right. Seven forty-five, then. Thank you. Good night, Mr.—"

His fingers covered her mouth swiftly, smothering the rest. "*Don't* say it," he warned. "Not unless you're prepared to take the consequences."

Her lips were warm, soft and moist beneath his fingers. He felt them tremble. Looking deeply into her widened eyes, he noted that she knew exactly what he threatened. And that some small, reluctant part of her was tempted.

Something else for him to think about during the night.

He pulled his hand away very slowly. "Now, what were you saying?" he asked with a supreme attempt at nonchalance.

She cleared her throat. "Good night, Rhys."

He smiled his approval. "Good night, Angelique."

She didn't bolt from the car to her house. Not exactly, he told himself as he backed out of the driveway after watching until she was safely inside.

Angelique St. Clair was afraid of him, he mused as he lay in bed hours later. Not in the office; she'd never been intimidated by him as an employer. But on a personal level, he scared her to death.

Which had to mean that she was as attracted to him as he was to her. And just as wary of that attraction.

He wasn't even aware that he was smiling when he finally slipped into sleep.

5

RHYS WAS AMUSED to note the expression on Angie's face when she answered her door to him the next morning. She couldn't have looked more coolly professional had she worn a uniform, which she had, in a manner of speaking. Her gray suit was so severe it wouldn't have been out of place in a convent; her soft gold hair had been pulled so tightly back from her face that her cheekbones looked more prominent than usual. Her chin was squared, her shoulders so straight he could have balanced glasses of water on them.

"Good morning, Angelique."

Her lashes flickered just perceptibly and then she answered blandly. "Good morning, Rhys." She stepped out, shutting her door behind her. "Thank you again for picking me up this morning."

"You're quite welcome," he replied smoothly, motioning for her to precede him to the car. He could be equally cool and businesslike, he thought in wry amusement. If this was the way she wanted to play it, he'd go along. For now.

Her stubbornly maintained poise wavered only once that day, when Rhys informed her that he'd had her car towed to a reliable garage for a full overhaul. "You did that without consulting me?" she asked him in startled displeasure.

"Yes," he answered simply, turning a page of the market report he was perusing.

"Rhys, why did you do that?" she demanded, audibly perturbed. "I can't afford a complete overhaul! The car's probably not even worth what this will cost."

"Don't worry about that. It'll be taken care of."

The silence stretched so long that he looked up from the report to study her expression. If the flames in those violet eyes were real, he reflected with interest, he would be well roasted. "Now what's the problem?"

"I don't want you paying for my car repairs," she answered bluntly.

"I have no intention of paying for your car repairs. The company is paying." His voice was even, firm. Slightly annoyed employer speaking to recalcitrant subordinate. "As my assistant, it is imperative that you have reliable transportation. Since this is such a new position, I hadn't thought to authorize a company vehicle for your use. As of today, you'll be driving a company car. I don't care what you do with your other one, drive it occasionally, sell it, whatever you like. The company car is for your use, both professional and personal. It's one of the perks of your position. If you decide to move on, the next person to fill your office will receive the same benefits. Does that satisfy your outraged virtue, Ms. St. Clair?"

Her cheeks reddened, but her chin didn't lower even fractionally. "As you wish, Mr. Wakefield."

He nodded curtly and turned his eyes back downward. "Get Henderson on the phone," he ordered. "Set up a meeting for sometime next week. Tell him I want him to come fully prepared this time."

"Yes, sir." She turned and opened the door, then paused.

He looked up. "Something else?"

She didn't quite meet his eyes. He couldn't help remembering the morning before, when he'd reluctantly offered the apology he knew she deserved. He must have been wearing very much the same expression then that she wore now. "About the car," she murmured. "Thank you."

"You're welcome, Angelique. Go call Henderson."

She didn't linger. Staring absently at the door she'd closed behind her, Rhys chuckled, shook his head and went back to work, wondering if he'd ever completely understand his lovely, spirited assistant.

RHYS FOLLOWED HIS USUAL routine during the next few weeks. First to arrive at the office, last to leave. There were no further conflicts between him and Angie, no intimate interludes. No more invitations to dinner. He considered himself biding his time, waiting to see what would happen. If Angie was aware that Rhys was only temporarily indulging her obvious desire to maintain a strictly professional relationship, she didn't show it. Outwardly nothing had changed between them on that Friday he'd taken ill.

Even Rhys couldn't have explained why he'd altered his route to work and home after finding out where Angie lived. He never failed now to drive past her house, no matter how early or how late the hour. He learned a few more things about her simply by studying her house as he drove past. The plain, functional company car he'd assigned her was usually in the driveway. As far as he could tell, she never had visitors. The lights were always on in the house when he passed in the evenings, unless he'd lingered so long at the office that she'd already turned in for the night.

Even then, a small lamp burned in what he assumed was the living room.

Was his so-competent, so-independent assistant afraid of the dark?

He couldn't help wondering why she seemed so isolated. His curiosity about her was becoming so intense that he was having a hard time containing it. He'd even considered having her investigated, though his conscience rebelled at such a blatant invasion of privacy. But it wasn't simply curiosity. He was beginning to worry about her—something he found almost staggering. He'd never worried about another person, with the exception of Aunt Iris, who'd been in increasingly poor health during the past few years.

What had happened to Angelique to turn her into such a recluse? He'd noted that she was beginning to make a few friends at the office, but she was still very much alone at home. He knew full well that she was not a natural loner, such as himself. Something traumatic had occurred in her life, something so shattering that he could still see the haunted look in her eyes in unguarded moments, even now, six months after he'd first met her. What could it have been?

Was she lonely? Frightened? Had it been a man who'd hurt her so deeply? And, most importantly it seemed, was there a man somewhere who still had a claim on her? That was the question that nagged him in the early hours of morning when he lay sleepless, tormented by images of her.

He wouldn't be able to continue this way much longer. No matter how firmly she held him at a distance, no matter how hard he tried to control his desire for her, the tension between them was building, strengthening. Sooner or later, something was going to give. In some ways, he looked forward to that point, eager to find out what would happen. In others, he dreaded it, wondering if either of them would survive the explosion intact.

"...SO THEIR OPINION is that we need to expand more into the medical equipment market to take up the slack caused by falling sales to the oil industry. With very few changes in the production line, the equipment we've been manufacturing can be converted for use in hospitals and..."

Though she listened attentively to every word Rhys was telling her, Angie found part of her mind captivated by the way the indirect office lighting gleamed in his thick silver hair. They sat side by side on the long sofa at one end of his office, where they'd been for the past half hour or so as they'd gone over the notes from the meeting held that morning with members of upper management and representatives of an outside consulting firm. It always seemed to help Rhys sort things out in his mind by discussing them aloud with her; she considered being a good listener an integral part of her job. She wondered who he'd talked to before he'd hired her.

"What do *you* think?"

That question got her full attention. She couldn't remember ever hearing him ask it before. "You want *my* opinion?"

Rhys frowned. "That was what I asked. You do have opinions, don't you?"

"Of course. You've just never seemed interested in them before," she answered bluntly.

His mouth twitched with the half smile she was coming to anticipate more all the time. "Most people don't wait to be asked before telling me how they think I should run my business."

"You hired me as your assistant, remember? If you'd wanted someone who'd felt qualified to run your business, you'd have hired one of those smart-ass M.B.A.s who wanted my job."

Rhys narrowed his eyes at her, the crease in his cheek that was almost a dimple deepening, though his smile did not. "No, I got me a smart-ass former social secretary, instead. It's been over a month since that particular outburst. Are you ever going to let me live it down?"

She laughed. "Probably not."

Rhys looked at her for so long that her smile faded and she shifted uncomfortably on the couch. "You've got a nice laugh," he said at length. "You should do it more often." And then he nodded abruptly toward the thick sheaf of notes on the low cocktail table in front of them. "So what do you think about the consultants' suggestions?"

Shaken by the expression she'd seen in his eyes before he'd turned away, Angie struggled to clear her thoughts sufficiently to answer with some semblance of intelligence. It seemed very important to justify Rhys's belief that her opinions held value. So why had her mind suddenly gone blank? Why had he chosen that particular moment to look at her as though he wanted to throw her over his shoulder and carry her away?

She was both relieved and astonished when the door to Rhys's office suddenly burst open, sparing her the need to speak. No one ever came into Rhys's office unannounced, without knocking. Not even his secretary. So who...?

The man didn't simply walk through the door. He exploded into the office in a whirl of red hair, white teeth and boisterous laughter. Angie sat stunned as the maniac attacked her employer, slapping him on the shoulder with enough force to nearly send him sprawling, greeting him with just-short-of-obscene insults.

She was even more shocked that Rhys didn't seem to mind the assault, even seemed pleased. Staring at him, she watched as the broad smile spread across his face—a smile that jolted her all the way to her toes, even though it wasn't turned on her. Oh, heavens, she thought faintly. If Rhys ever *should* happen to smile at her like that, she'd be a goner.

"What are you doing in town?" Rhys demanded of the stranger, who was so tall and powerfully built that he actually made six-foot, one-hundred-eighty-five-pound Rhys look small.

"Business. I'd have called first, but it was a spur-of-the-moment thing. Couldn't stop in Birmingham without seeing you, though."

"Damn straight. You knew I'd have your head if I found out you'd been in town without stopping to say hello," Rhys retorted easily. And then he seemed to remember Angie. He turned to look at her, and actually flushed a bit at the amazed expression on her face. He brushed back the lock of hair his friend's exuberant greeting had shaken onto his forehead. "Graham, I want you to meet someone. This is my assistant, Angelique St. Clair. Angelique, this is Graham Keating, an old army buddy."

"It's very nice to meet you, Mr. Keating," Angie said politely, extending her hand.

Her fingers disappeared into a paw the size of a dinner plate. "Well, well, well," Graham Keating murmured, subjecting her to a long, slow, minute inspection. "Well."

"As you can tell, Graham's quite a conversationalist," Rhys observed dryly.

"Shut up, Rhys." Graham never took his eyes away from Angie as he spoke mildly, nor did he release her hand. "So how'd a nice girl like you end up working for a nasty son of a gun like him, Angelique?"

"Angie," Rhys corrected before Angie could answer the teasing question. She glanced at him in question, but he continued to look at Graham. "Everyone calls her 'Angie.'"

Everyone but you, Angie added silently.

"The name fits," Graham mused, lifting his free hand to lightly touch Angie's hair. "The face and hair of an angel. I'd like to paint you sometime."

Rhys snorted in disgust, beginning to scowl. "Paint? The only thing you've ever painted is the outside of a barn, and you made a mess of that."

"Shut up, Rhys. I'm in the middle of a seduction here."

That was twice the man had told Rhys Wakefield to shut up, Angie reflected. And he was still standing. Amazing.

She tugged lightly at her hand, only to find herself pulled even closer to Rhys's eccentric friend. "So, Angel-face, how'd you like to have dinner with me tonight? I'm in town by myself—I'll be hungry and all alone. Won't you take pity on a visitor to your town?"

It was impossible not to like the guy. The laughter dancing in his candid green eyes was contagious. He was an attractive man, with his mane of copper hair and cleanly carved features. And yet she couldn't help comparing him to Rhys—and Rhys was by far the more fascinating of the two, in her opinion. She opened her mouth to politely decline the dinner invitation, but again was forestalled by Rhys.

A heavy arm fell around her shoulders, tugging her backward. She found herself plastered to Rhys's side before she quite knew how it happened. Staring up at him in surprise, she noted that his scowl had deepened, his smile gone completely. "Sorry, Graham, but she's not available—for dinner *or* seduction. Off-limits, you copy?" Though the words were spoken lightly enough, there was no mistaking the firm note of warning in his voice.

Graham looked from Rhys to Angie, then back again. "Coming through loud and clear, buddy. And it's about damned time!" With characteristic enthusiasm, he threw an arm around Rhys's shoulders, then included Angie in the near-strangling hug. "I have to compliment you on your taste, Rhys. She's a treasure. Beauty and brains. You make him treat you right, you hear, Angie? Let me know if he gets too obnoxious and I'll cut him down to size for you."

He released them abruptly. "Gotta go. I'm supposed to be in a meeting in less than half an hour on the other side of town. See you next time, buddy."

"Graham, wait," Rhys called out as his friend whirled for the door. "Why don't you plan to have dinner with us later?"

"Can't. Gotta get back to Houston tonight. Thanks for asking, though."

Rhys cocked his head quizzically. "Then what was that drivel about being all alone and hungry tonight?"

Graham grinned cockily. "Oh, that. I just wanted to see what you'd do if I made a play for your lady. I knew you'd staked a claim the minute I walked in. You were about to go for my throat, weren't you? It's about damned time," he repeated as he walked out and closed the door behind him.

Angie and Rhys stood frozen in position for a moment, and then she pulled away from him. "*What* was that?" she demanded, feeling as if she'd survived a tornado.

Grimacing ruefully, Rhys ran a hand through his hair and attempted a smile. "*That* was a crazy man. He's loud and tactless, chauvinistic and sometimes arrogant. He's also generous, softhearted, brave and trustworthy. He's the best friend I've ever had. Just about the only friend," he added candidly.

Touched by his words, Angie almost softened, and then she stiffened again. "Why in the world did you want your friend to think that you and I—that we—"

Rhys cleared his throat when her voice trailed off for lack of an appropriate phrase. Shoving his hands in his pockets, he shrugged. "I was—uh—trying to protect you."

"Protect me from what?" Angie asked in disbelief.

"Well, I'm very fond of Graham, of course, but he's a bit of a womanizer. Terrible reputation."

Temper building, Angie planted her hands on her hips and glared at him, foot tapping irritably on the plush carpeting. "And just who asked you to protect me—from Graham or anything else? You allowed your friend to believe that you and I are involved in an affair, Rhys, and I don't appreciate that at all! I am perfectly capable of taking care of myself. Besides," she added, growing more angry by the minute, "for all you knew, I *wanted* to go out with him! Maybe I was going to say yes to his invita—"

Even in her unwelcome fantasies, Angie had never

realized quite how powerful Rhys Wakefield's kiss would be. She hadn't even seen him move. Yet now she found herself gripped tightly in his arms, his mouth moving forcefully on hers. There wasn't much she could do except clutch his lapels and hold on as she was whirled into the middle of a second, even more mind-spinning tornado than the one Graham had brought with him into the formerly quiet office.

The embrace was rough and showed little evidence of smooth, practiced skill, but the underlying hunger and passion devastated her. She'd *never* been kissed like this. With a muffled moan, her lips opened to his insistent tongue, and she was unable to prevent herself from responding to the kiss with a helpless desire of her own. She'd been fantasizing about this moment for too long.

His body was hard and warm through his tailored suit. The body she'd seen in such detail in his bedroom. The body that had haunted her ever since. She hadn't even begun to imagine how incredible it would feel pressed against hers.

His mouth was hot, clever, surprisingly soft. She hadn't known how wonderful he would taste.

His hands were firm, strong, possessive. They swept her back in long, slow arcs, leaving her aching and quivering in their wake. She wanted more.

Her building desire finally gave her the strength to pull away from him before she did something utterly foolish. She stood staring at Rhys, and he at her, for a long, tense moment. And then she finally, unsteadily managed one word, "Why?"

Rhys's voice was gruff. "If you didn't realize that's been building from the beginning, then you're not quite as intelligent as I've been giving you credit for."

His words—and the look in his eyes—had her backing frantically away. "Rhys, no. I don't want this. We can't—"

"I think we already are."

Her hands came up instinctively, palms toward him as if to ward him off. "No. I can't afford to get involved with you. Not in that sort of way. I work for you. I want to keep it at that."

His strong chin lifting, Rhys glowered at her, obviously stung by her near panic. "You can relax, Angelique. I've never forced myself on a woman before and I'm not going to begin with you. You wanted that kiss as badly as I did. You responded—fully."

"It can't happen again," she said, her voice gaining strength, steadier now. "Not if I'm going to continue to work for you."

"I suppose that's up to you."

He looked so distant, she thought, studying him gravely. So isolated. Much as he had the first time she'd seen him. She hadn't realized until now how his manner had softened toward her during the past six months. Now that she thought about it, she hadn't noticed his attitude changing toward anyone else. Only to her—and to the man he'd called his only friend. A curious pang of loss shot through her. One she had to ignore. She couldn't afford to indulge in an affair with her boss. She'd suffered too many losses in her life lately to deliberately flirt with another, potentially more devastating one.

"I hope that we'll be able to work together as we always have, that we'll be able to put this behind us," she said quietly.

"I see no reason why we shouldn't," he replied coolly. He turned away, his profile unreadable. "As a matter of fact, there's quite a bit that needs to be done now. I want you to set up a meeting with all the department heads. Have June type these notes and make copies for everyone. Get me some cost figures together from engineering and have them included in the report. And, while you're at it..."

Angie listened attentively to the rest of the instructions, her face expressionless. She was certain that no one could tell by looking at her that her heart had just suffered a painful bruise. If she could hurt this badly now, then she'd been justified in calling a halt before things had progressed any further.

"And, Ms. St. Clair—"

"Yes, sir?" she asked steadily, though her throat constricted sharply at his return to icy formality. She hadn't realized how much she'd come to relish being called "Angelique" by him until he'd stopped.

"Don't dawdle. These decisions have to be made quickly."

"Yes, sir." She turned abruptly and left his office, her eyes burning with tears she'd love to shed if only there was someplace private to do so.

Left alone, Rhys stood in one spot for a long, brooding moment before he turned and slammed his fist against the closest wall.

And then he sat down at his desk, and very deliberately picked up the telephone to call an investigator he'd had cause to employ a time or two in the past few years. He was tired of battling an unknown enemy. He intended to find out exactly what he was up against with Angelique St. Clair.

RHYS LEFT TOWN the next week to pursue a series of meetings concerning the impending shift in corporate operations. Angie was left with the responsibility of overseeing his office, handling what she could, contacting Rhys if he was needed, holding anything else until his return. She welcomed both the work and his absence. She hoped the time apart would give her a chance to recover her equilibrium, something she hadn't been able to do since that kiss.

The tension between them had been painfully uncomfortable, though they'd both been very careful not to let it interfere with their work. He'd been civil enough to her, but his cool formality had only reminded her more forcefully of the heat of the embrace they'd shared. She missed the tentative closeness that had developed between them, the shared smiles and easy conversation. She missed *him*.

She wasn't sleeping well, had little appetite. She was generally miserable. She was even beginning to consider looking for another job, though she doubted she'd find another as prestigious or well paying as this one. She couldn't imagine anyone else taking the kind of risk with her that Rhys had taken in hiring her. But how could she continue to work for him when she had the terrible suspicion that she was hovering on the edge of falling in love with him? And how could she keep her distance from him when he had only to give her a slight half smile or say her name to make her melt at his feet?

Though she told herself she was glad he was gone, by Wednesday his office seemed so painfully empty that she found dozens of excuses not to enter it. She used June shamefully, calling upon the secretary to bring her the materials she needed from Rhys's office, claiming she was too inundated with work to fetch them herself. She tried to make up for her behavior by being especially nice to the other woman, who warmed fully under the attention Angie paid her.

A good-natured, extroverted woman, June seemed to grow genuinely fond of Angie, even bringing her a couple of fresh, homemade blueberry muffins on Thursday morning with the motherly expostulation that Angie was getting too thin. "Don't let Mr. Wakefield work you down to skin and bones, honey," she added kindly. "You let him know you're only human and you need time to rest and to eat, you hear?"

Only human. Boy, was she ever, Angie thought even as she thanked June for her concern and for the muffins. She wondered what the older woman would say if she knew that Angie was suffering from a severe case of lust for their formidable employer.

Rhys called that afternoon to discuss the progress of his meetings and give Angie a list of instructions. The conversation was brief, clipped, productive. It ended without ceremony. Rhys seemed to go out of his way not to address her personally, though she was perversely relieved that he didn't call her "Ms. St. Clair" in the distant, rather sarcastic voice he'd used after their confrontation in his office.

She was horrified to realize that tears were rolling down her cheeks when the call ended. She dashed her hand across her face, determined that no one would see what a mess she was becoming, determined to get herself back in hand.

Angie was playing on the floor with Flower when her doorbell rang early that evening. Her hand freezing on the rapidly growing kitten's rumbling tummy, she jerked her head to stare at the door as if she could tell by looking at it who stood on the other side. What if it were—?

No, it couldn't be. Rhys wasn't due back in town until early the next afternoon. And even if he'd arrived earlier than anticipated, he wouldn't come here. Would he?

She wasn't at all sure if she was relieved or disappointed that her caller was her young neighbor, Mickey. "Well, hi. What's up?" she asked, effortlessly returning the boy's bright grin.

"I got a new watch. My mom said I could come show it to you. Ain't it cool? It's got a calculator and a stopwatch and it tells the time and the date and everything. It's even got an alarm and it beeps every hour. My grandpa got it for me."

Angie dutifully admired the multi-buttoned digital watch. "That *is* cool," she assured him. "Would you like to come in, Mickey?"

"Yeah, thanks, but my mom said I couldn't stay long. Where's—oh, there she is. Hi, Flower." Mickey darted past Angie to kneel on the floor and roughhouse with the playful kitten. "She's really growing, ain't she?"

Resisting the impulse to correct his grammar, Angie nodded. "Yes, she is. Not surprising, as much as she eats. You didn't tell me she had four hollow legs."

Mickey laughed. "That's what my mom says about me. Well, not four, I only got two, but I'm hungry all the time." He eyed the kitchen door as he spoke.

Taking the hint, Angie asked politely, "Would you like a cookie?"

Mickey's grin broadened to show all four gaps where teeth had once been. "You bet."

"Have you had your dinner yet?"

"I had a hot dog and some chips. Mom's making

some kind of fancy French stuff for her and Dad and Grandpa, but she said I didn't have to eat it."

"That was very understanding of her," Angie replied, leading the boy to the kitchen table and handing him two chocolate chip cookies and a glass of milk.

"Mmm. She's okay," Mickey agreed offhandedly. "Most of the time." He stuffed half a cookie into his mouth, eyeing Angie curiously as he chewed and swallowed. "You're not sick or anything, are you, Angie?" he asked when his mouth was relatively empty.

"No, I'm fine," she answered, startled. "Why do you ask?"

"I dunno. You look kinda funny," Mickey returned with a shrug. He swallowed the remaining half of the cookie, then picked up the other. "How come there's never anyone but you here, Angie? Don't you got any friends?"

"You're my friend." Angie was quite proud that her smile didn't waver. "And I've made some friends at my office."

"Don't you ever get lonely?"

"Yes, sometimes," she admitted candidly. "I suppose everyone gets lonely sometimes when they live alone. That's why I enjoy your visits so much."

The doorbell rang again before Mickey could respond. "That'll be my mom," he guessed, rolling his eyes.

She smiled. "Let's go see."

Mickey was right. His mother waited at the door. "Is he making a terrible pest of himself?" she asked ruefully.

"Not at all. I was just telling him how much I enjoy his visits." Angie had met Mickey's mother, Kim, several times and liked the woman, though they'd spent little time together.

"You're very patient with him. He can be a handful." Kim motioned for Mickey to join her outside. "C'mon, Mick. Your grandpa wants to spend more time with you while he's visiting."

She paused, then tilted her head at Angie. "Angie, would you like to join us for dinner tomorrow night? We'd love to have you."

"Thank you, but I can't tomorrow night. There's a retirement party for one of the vice presidents at my office and I'm obligated to be there."

"Another time, then?"

"Yes, I'd love to," Angie accepted rather shyly. "Thank you for asking."

"I'll give you a call. Let's go, Mickey."

Mickey hesitated, then threw his arms around Angie's waist for an impulsive hug. "Thanks for the cookies, Angie. See you later, okay?"

Knowing the hug was prompted by his concern about her being lonely, Angie returned it warmly. She closed the door slowly behind the child and his mother, thinking of how long it had been since she'd been hugged. How very good it felt. She couldn't help wondering wistfully if she'd ever have her own child to hug. The prospect didn't look too promising at the moment.

She told herself it was only coincidence that her very next thought was of Rhys. She'd be seeing him again the next afternoon. She told herself that she was ready, that she had everything under control now. And then she tried to prepare dinner with her fingers crossed for luck.

6

RHYS STOOD in Angie's open doorway for several moments before she looked up from her work to spot him there. He took advantage of the opportunity to drink in the sight of her. He hadn't forgotten how beautiful she was, but he'd never grow tired of looking at her.

She'd worn her hair down that day, soft and loose to her shoulders, something she rarely did. Even her dress was more casual than usual, a splash of cheerful pastels that brought out the soft pink in her complexion. He supposed she'd come prepared to attend Atwood's retirement party after work. Probably assumed—correctly—that they'd be so busy catching up from his week away that they'd work right up until the party began, giving her no chance to go home and change.

He'd missed her during the long week apart. He hadn't realized how much a part of his life she'd become in the past six months or so.

A securely sealed brown envelope had been lying on his desk when he'd returned, marked "personal." There'd been no return address, but he'd known who it was from when he'd ripped into it. He'd paused momentarily before reading the cleanly typed report inside, but he hadn't changed his mind. He needed to find out about Angie's past, needed to know what demons were chasing her. Needed to know why she felt the need to stay so alone and whether he had the slightest chance of changing her mind.

So now he knew. His eyes on her gleaming hair as she bent so diligently over her work, Rhys wavered between taking her in his arms and turning her over his knee. Did she really think it mattered that her father was in prison? He knew she'd been completely exonerated of her father's shady dealings, that she'd been guilty of nothing more than filial ignorance. Did she honestly believe that he or anyone else would hold something like that against her after knowing what a fine person she was in her own right?

He wished he could tell her those things, but he knew he couldn't. Not yet. Now wasn't the time to let her know what he'd done. Not until he had her full trust. And he would have it eventually. One way or another.

"Hello, Angelique."

Her head flew up with a jerk. He watched the color stain her fair cheeks, noted the gleam of memory and awareness in her unusual violet eyes. "Rhys," she said before she could remember to address him more formally.

He was fiercely glad that she'd called him by name. She noticed what she'd said a moment after he did, but only a flick of her lashes betrayed her discomfiture. "How was your flight?" she asked evenly.

"Fine. You look beautiful today. I like your hair down."

She obviously hadn't expected that. He watched her moisten her lips, feeling his chest tighten at the unconscious eroticism of the gesture. Those lips had haunted him for over a week now. He could almost taste them in his sleep as he replayed their kiss again and again in his dreams.

"Um—thank you."

"You're welcome. Do you have time now to get me caught up on everything that went on here during the week?"

"Yes, sir. Just let me get my notes."

"I'll wait for you in my office."

"I'll be right there."

He smiled at her. "Take your time. We have all afternoon."

He almost laughed at the wariness in her eyes as she nodded slowly in response. She didn't quite know what to make of his renewed friendliness. He rather liked seeing her off guard this way.

Rhys made no further efforts at intimacy during the long, busy afternoon. His game was one of advance and retreat, designed to lull her into a partial sense of security. Something told him that it would be all too easy to go too far, causing her to bolt in sheer panic.

As both of them had expected, their work kept them busy until the moment the party began downstairs. Angie slipped away before Rhys was able to do so. Some fifteen minutes later, Rhys followed her down, wondering if she'd been reluctant to make an appearance at his side.

Patience, he counseled himself, swallowing his exasperation with her. *Be patient, Rhys. Your time will come.*

ANGIE WAS RATHER PLEASED by the welcome she received at the retirement party when she entered a few minutes late. She wasn't sure when it had happened, but she had become an accepted member of the staff. Even the three men from engineering whom she had turned down for dates greeted her with friendly smiles. One of them offered to get her a drink. She thanked him, then explained that she preferred nonalcoholic drinks.

He smiled, his dark eyes glittering. "No problem. There's a fruit drink that I think you'll like. It's really very good."

"Thank you," she accepted with a smile. "That would be very nice." And then she was distracted when Gay and Darla approached with husbands in tow for introductions. When the engineer returned with her fruit drink, Angie was in the middle of a laughing, boisterous group, rapidly gaining confidence as she joined in the banter.

The drink obtained for her was delicious. Since she hadn't had time to grab a bite of anything since breakfast, she welcomed the pulpy beverage, hoping she'd be able to gracefully attack the snack table a little later. When a second glass was pressed into her hand after she'd finished the first, she took it gratefully, still too involved in conversation to pay much attention to the smug looks being exchanged by the three engineers.

Even as she chatted with her co-workers, she was vividly aware that Rhys was watching her from across the room where he stood in conversation with a couple of the vice presidents. She felt his eyes on her almost as if he were physically touching her. She couldn't read his mood today, but there'd been no mistaking the expression she'd spied in his eyes once or twice. Desire. Rhys Wakefield had decided he wanted her. And Rhys Wakefield was a man who usually got what he wanted.

Trying desperately, unsuccessfully, to ignore him, she took another large gulp of her fruit drink.

RHYS WASN'T FOND of parties. He attended them only when necessary, as it was tonight. His usual practice was to make an appearance, say a few appropriate words and then tactfully disappear. Tonight, however, he lingered, watching Angie.

She was so damned beautiful. And he wasn't the only one who noticed. Every single man in the room— and some of the married ones—had drifted her way at some point during the evening. It occurred to him that she was mingling much more easily with her co-workers now than she had in the beginning. She'd tried to hold them at arm's length but hadn't been successful. She was too naturally outgoing to remain aloof for long. Sooner or later she would realize that her father's mistakes didn't matter, and then she'd be ready to rejoin the social scene she'd left.

He didn't try to fool himself into believing that she'd turn to him when that happened. He had very little to offer her. He was too old for her, too much the loner, totally inept when it came to personal relationships. But he'd become increasingly aware that he wouldn't rest until he'd had her, at least for a little while. If she could turn to him now, while she was still lonely and hurting, if he could offer her anything—well, then maybe it wouldn't be so bad when she moved on. Maybe.

Atwood, the honoree of the party, stopped to thank Rhys for the tribute, as well as the customary gold watch. Rhys wished the long-time employee, who'd been with the company for many years before Rhys had acquired it, the best of luck in his retirement, asking courteously about the older man's plans. When Rhys glanced back in Angie's direction, he frowned as he noted the suspicious behavior of the three engineers who'd hardly left her side for the past hour.

What was going on? And just what was in the frosted glasses they were eagerly fetching for her? Knowing his assistant's policy about alcohol, he decided he'd better investigate.

He was detained before he'd taken more than a few steps. Trying not to be rude, he answered a question from the personnel director and then stopped to listen to something a supervisor from Research and Development wanted brought to his attention. "See me first thing Monday morning and we'll discuss this," he instructed as soon as he had the opportunity.

By the time he'd made his way across the room, several more minutes had passed. His attention on Angie, Rhys realized that he'd been right about his suspicions. Her eyes were slightly glazed, her cheeks rather flushed, her laughter too bright. His cool, competent assistant was more than a little inebriated, though she seemed to be handling it amazingly well. He approached in time to hear her cheerfully declining an invitation from one of the engineers to drive her home. By the time Rhys reached her side, another one had tried and been pleasantly shot down.

So, he thought with a tug of satisfaction, Angelique wasn't quite the easy drunk she'd feared herself to be.

He touched her shoulder. "Having a nice time?" he asked quietly.

"Oh, yes, lovely," she replied with a vague smile. "Are you?"

"Mmm." He turned his attention to the engineers, who were starting to sidle away, looking a bit concerned. They stopped dead when he spoke to them. "Perhaps Ms. St. Clair forgot to mention to you that she doesn't drink?" he inquired blandly, nodding to the insidiously innocent-looking concoction one of them had been prepared to give her as soon as she'd finished the one in her hand. The stricken looks he received in answer confirmed his suspicion that she had, and that the three had been amusing themselves by getting the always-so-cool-and-dignified executive assistant tipsy.

"Oh, I told them, Rh—Mr. Wakefield," Angie assured him, lightly touching his arm. "This is just a fruit drink."

He covered her hand with his, still glaring at his rather pale subordinates. "I'm afraid some of that fruit has fermented, Ms. St. Clair. I believe your friends here have been playing a little joke on you."

Angie looked at the nearly empty glass in her hand and then at the three men standing miserably in front of her. She raised a not-quite-steady hand to her temple. "And I thought I was beginning to feel dizzy from lack of food," she moaned.

"That probably had something to do with it," he agreed. Spotting his secretary standing with her husband a few feet away, he motioned her over. "Ms. St. Clair isn't feeling well," he explained. "Would you mind seeing her to the lobby and waiting with her there for a moment? I'll be taking her home."

"Yes, Mr. Wakefield. Come on, honey, I'll help you out," June offered immediately, taking Angie's arm. "Goodness, you look pale. I just knew you've been working yourself too hard this week," she scolded gently, leading her charge away. "Didn't I tell you you have to take better care of yourself?"

Rhys waited until Angie was out of hearing before signaling the three wretched engineers to follow him to a relatively private corner. Aware of the speculative looks of the other guests of the party, he kept his voice low as he told them in a few pithy words exactly what he thought of their sophomoric stunt. By the time he was finished, all three were relieved that they still had their jobs. Pausing only long enough to say his good-byes to Atwood, Rhys left the party immediately afterward.

June was still scolding when Rhys collected Angie in the lobby. "You're both alike," she accused her employer. "All work, no relaxation. You may have learned how to live that way, but Ms. St. Clair isn't quite as tough as you. You're both going to have to start taking care of yourselves. See that she gets something to eat tonight, you hear?"

"I will. Thanks, June."

"Oh, don't mention it, Mr. Wakefield. Good night, Ms. St. Clair. Get some rest, okay?"

Her eyes heavy lidded, swaying a bit on her feet, Angie managed a weak smile. "Good night, June. Thank you." She turned her smile to Rhys when he took her arm in a steadying grip. Leaning trustingly against him, she rested her head for a moment against his forearm. "I'm really tired, Rhys," she murmured. "And I feel like an idiot. Take me home, please."

"Don't worry about it, Boston," he replied bracingly, slipping an arm around her waist to steady her. "You didn't know what was going on. Where's your purse?"

"Here it is." Rhys almost winced at the speculative look in his secretary's eyes when she held out the leather bag. And then she smiled brightly in what he could only assume was approval. "You take good care of her, now."

"Good night, June."

"Good night, Mr. Wakefield."

RHYS HELPED ANGIE into his car and buckled her in, trying to keep his touch impersonal as he leaned across her, his cheek only inches from her breasts. Clearing his throat, he straightened, shut her door and walked around the front of the car, wondering how long he could continue to be so damned noble. Climbing behind the wheel, he tried to think of something innocuous to say as he started the car and backed out of the parking space. He needn't have bothered. By the time he'd left the company parking lot, Angie had snuggled into the soft leather upholstery and fallen sound asleep.

Casting speculative sideways glances as he drove, Rhys noticed for the first time that she seemed to have lost weight in the past few weeks. By her own admission, she hadn't been eating well. And she was sleeping so soundly now, despite the movement of the car and her uncomfortable position. Could it be that she had been sleeping no better than he had lately? Had her nights been disturbed by memories of the kiss they'd shared, by fantasies of carrying that embrace to its natural conclusion? Or was he indulging in wistful thinking?

He drove past the turnoff to her house without even slowing down. He supposed he should take her home, but he had no intention of leaving her alone like this.

She hardly stirred when he lifted her out of the car and carried her into his house. She was so small, he mused, taking her upstairs with very little effort. Snuggled into his shoulder, her hand curled trustingly on his chest, she seemed very fragile, very delicate. Some strong, rather primitive emotion surged through him. Laying her carefully on his bed, he attempted to analyse it. Protectiveness, he decided at length, smoothing her silky hair away from her pale, still face. It wasn't an emotion he quite knew how to handle, wasn't one she'd appreciate, independent young woman that she was. But still, that's what he felt as he stood looking down at her. Almost as if she were his to protect.

He slipped her shoes off, then hesitated before covering her. The pastel dress, lovely as it was, hardly looked like comfortable sleepwear. As if in confirmation of that thought, she stirred against the pillow, her forehead creasing into the slightest hint of a frown before smoothing again in sleep. Steeling himself, Rhys lifted her enough to grasp her zipper and ease it downward. He held his breath as he slipped the dress down her arms and off her hips. She stirred again, but didn't protest. He wasn't quite as gentle when he stripped away her panty hose, his control rapidly dissipating. Nobility didn't suit him very well, he thought rather grimly.

He couldn't resist taking one long look at her before covering her with the crisp blue sheet. She was exquisite. Her skin was creamy, flawless, her legs long, smooth. She would burn easily, he mused, noting her fairness, but then a tan would be nothing short of criminal on such porcelain perfection. The two scraps of pink lace she wore for underwear hid very little from his hungry eyes, but it wasn't hard to imagine the beauty they concealed. His imagination was proving quite inconvenient at the moment, urging his body into an arousal that was nothing short of painful. Biting off a groan, he pulled up the sheet, leaning over her to tuck in the other side.

She murmured something and then her heavy lashes lifted, her eyes a bit glazed as they stared into his from only scant inches away. The last time they'd been in this position it had been he in this bed, he remembered, and she leaning over him. He'd wanted to kiss her then. He ached to kiss her now.

"What are you doing?" she asked, the words rather slurred.

"Tucking you in," he answered roughly. "Go back to sleep, Angelique."

But he didn't straighten immediately, and she looked at his mouth for a moment before raising her eyes slowly back to his. "Are you going to kiss me goodnight?"

Desire slammed through him so violently it nearly brought him to his knees. He cleared his throat. "I was thinking about it."

"Oh." She seemed to consider it for a moment, then smiled and lifted her face in invitation. "What's taking you so long?"

He stopped himself only a breath away from her parted lips. "This is a really bad idea."

"No. You kiss spectacularly, Rhys. Has anyone ever told you that?"

His mouth went dry. "Not lately."

Her hand slipped behind his head, tugging lightly. "Kiss me, Rhys."

"If you remember this in the morning, you'll probably go for my throat," he muttered, resisting for a moment longer.

She looked puzzled. "But I'm *asking* you to," she pointed out.

"Mmm. Something tells me that's not going to make a hell of a lot of difference."

She sighed wearily. "We'll worry about that tomorrow. Kiss me, Rhys."

Nobility was abruptly abandoned. It hadn't really

been his style, anyway, he thought just before his mouth closed over hers and his mind shut down completely. Almost without knowing how he'd accomplished it, he was beside her in the bed, their legs tangled with the sheet that separated them, arms interlaced, tongues feverishly entwined.

The kiss they'd shared before had been powerful, even with Angie holding back, resisting the temptation to participate fully. But her inhibitions were down now, weakened by alcohol and exhaustion. And they were in the intimacy of his bedroom rather than the more repressive surroundings of his office. This kiss almost made him whimper.

He'd known it would be like this. Somehow he'd known from the moment he'd looked up to find her sitting in front of his desk, her violet eyes wary as she'd waited for him to reject her application, her stubborn chin squared in rebellion against the anticipated rebuff. For six months he'd tried to remind himself of all the reasons this couldn't happen. For six months he'd tried to interest himself in other women, only to find his thoughts turning again and again to Angelique. For six long, frustrating months he'd wanted her, even as he'd told himself he couldn't have her.

And now she was in his arms, warm, willing, pliant. His for the taking. Triumph surged hotly through him, settling in the throbbing, feverish vicinity of his loins. Tonight he'd have her. Tonight he could stop torturing himself with fantasies, stop driving himself mad wondering if their joining would be as sensational as he imagined. Tonight he'd find out. Maybe—just maybe—he'd be able to let her walk away tomorrow, after he'd satisfied himself with her tonight. Maybe taking her would free him from his obsession with her.

His mouth moved avidly from her moist, trembling lips to her throat, sliding inexorably downward. She murmured her approval, holding him more tightly as she tilted her head back to better accommodate him. "Rhys," she whispered huskily. "Oh, Rhys."

His hand was on her breast. She filled his palm perfectly. He could almost taste her already as his mouth hovered above the straining lace-covered tip. She arched upward, offering herself trustingly to him.

Trustingly.

He hesitated, lowered his mouth a fraction of an inch more, then groaned and rolled away from her. "Hell."

Moaning her dismay, Angie reached for him again. "Rhys. Rhys, please."

Don't ask me like that, Angelique. He shoved himself off the bed as if the sheets were on fire. Not that he'd have been surprised if they had been after what had passed between them. "Go to sleep," he ordered harshly, refusing to look at her. "You don't want this."

"But—"

"Just go to sleep," he repeated, heading for the door with long, jerky strides. "I'll see you in the morning."

He didn't look back to see if she followed his advice. He walked out the door and straight down the stairs, needing a drink more than he could ever remember needing one before. It was a damned poor substitute for Angelique, but the best he could do at the moment.

He hated being noble, he thought savagely, pouring liquor into a glass with enough force to splatter every surface within two feet of him.

"OH, MY GOD." Angie sat up in the bed, her throbbing head clutched in unsteady hands as she made a valiant effort not to be sick. She was going to die, she thought miserably. She only hoped it would be soon.

When the worst of the pain set off by the mere action of sitting up had passed, she cautiously lowered her hands and opened her eyes to puffy slits. And then her lids flew up in horror as her surroundings finally came into focus. This was *not* her bedroom. But it was one she recognized. Groaning loudly enough to make her head start to pound again, she covered her face with her hands, quite certain she was going to be sick this time.

She was in Rhys Wakefield's bed, wearing nothing more than her underwear.

Those fruit drinks. Those damned delicious, refreshingly pulpy fruit drinks. What an idiot she'd been. What a stupid, trusting idiot.

Her fury with herself soon sought a more convenient outlet. The engineers. How dare they trick her that way, lie to her, amuse themselves at her expense? But it wasn't very satisfying to be enraged with people who weren't anywhere around. She needed someone she could yell at, someone close enough to provide a target for her frustrated anger. Someone like Rhys Wakefield.

Vague memories of hot, hungry kisses tormented her as she gingerly pulled on the dress she found neatly folded on the chair near the bed. Her right breast tingled with the memory of Rhys's touch. Unfortunately—or was it fortunately?—she could remember nothing more. How could he take advantage of her that way? And even more annoying, how could she have forgotten the details?

She intended to tell him exactly what she thought of a man who would take advantage of a woman's vulnerability—especially when he knew why she always tried to stay away from alcoholic beverages. She would speak her mind even if it meant losing her job. She was going to march right down those stairs and—

She stopped in the hallway when a glance through the open door opposite her let her know she had been on the verge of making a worse mistake than trusting the engineers at the party.

The bedroom across the hall from Rhys's was even more sparsely furnished than his, holding nothing more than a bed and a matching dresser. Sprawled across the bed, still fully dressed except for his shoes, Rhys slept soundly, facedown on the plain brown bedspread. Even in her muddled condition, it was glaringly obvious that he hadn't taken advantage of her the night before, as she'd been prepared to accuse him.

"Rhys. Rhys, please." The memory of her own husky voice pleading for his kisses—and more—made her wince in chagrin. Her hands over her burning cheeks, she realized that she must have all but thrown herself at him, but he had pulled away. Far from having the right to berate him, she owed him her gratitude. Which, for some reason, was even more galling.

Taking great care not to disturb him, she turned and walked back into the other bedroom, heading straight for the aspirin she knew he kept in the medicine cabinet in the adjoining bathroom. She washed two of them down with a paper cup of water, rinsed her mouth out, made a hasty effort of tidying her disheveled hair with her fingers and then opened the door, intending to call a cab. She hoped to make her escape before Rhys woke up, not caring that her escape would be somewhat less than gracious.

She'd taken two steps across the bedroom when

Rhys appeared in the doorway. "Good morning, Angelique."

People didn't really die from hangovers—*or* from embarrassment, she reminded herself as she answered with whatever dignity she could summon. "Good morning, Rhys."

He eyed her closely. "I won't ask how you're feeling. It's pretty obvious."

"Then I must look worse than I thought," she returned with an attempt at levity.

"You look fine," he assured her gravely. "A little pale."

"I hadn't realized you could be so diplomatic." She moistened her lips and turned away from him, her bare feet curling into the plush carpeting. "I don't suppose you've seen my shoes?"

"Under the bed. I was afraid you'd get up in the night and trip over them."

"Oh—uh—thanks." Knowing her face must be an interesting shade of crimson, she slowly started to bend down.

Rhys chuckled and reached out a hand to stop her. His fingers closing gently on her shoulder, he murmured, "I'll get them. I don't think your head can take it."

Gratefully she allowed him the gesture. She suspected that if she'd managed to get down there, she would never have been able to get back up without assistance. Surreptitiously rubbing one aching temple with her fingertips, she wondered how quickly she'd be able to make her escape.

"Have you taken anything for that headache?" Rhys asked when she'd slipped her feet into her practical pumps.

"Yes. I helped myself to a couple of aspirin from your medicine cabinet."

"They should start working soon. You'll feel better after you've eaten something."

Her stomach turned over. "I'm not hungry."

"Sure you are. You just don't know it yet." Taking her arm, he pulled her toward the doorway. "I'll make us some breakfast."

"No, really, Rhys. I couldn't eat a thing."

"When's the last time you ate?"

"I—uh—" She tried to remember. "I had breakfast yesterday. Half a bagel and some orange juice."

He snorted his disgust. "No wonder those drinks took you out so easily last night. Why the hell didn't you eat lunch? Or dinner?"

"At noon I was getting everything ready for your return to the office, and you and I worked together through dinner," she retorted defensively. "When's the last time *you* ate?"

He paused at the foot of the stairs, thinking. "I had breakfast yesterday," he admitted reluctantly. "But it was a bigger breakfast than yours."

She rolled her eyes. "Oh, that's much better," she drawled sarcastically.

He smiled, then laughed softly and shook his head. "We're quite a pair, aren't we? Come on, Boston, crawl into the bathroom, and I'll make us breakfast. I promise you won't be sick if you eat a little—from my cooking *or* your hangover. Trust me."

Trust him? How could she not after last night? He'd rescued her from certain humiliation, resisted when she'd begged him to make love to her. She told herself that it didn't really matter why he had resisted, but some tiny, intensely feminine part of her hoped he'd been trying to be noble. She'd really hate to think that he hadn't even been tempted.

She almost moaned in dismay as the thought crystallized in her mind. *Honestly, Angie, must you continue to make a fool of yourself over this man?* she demanded of herself in sheer exasperation, sitting meekly at the kitchen table as Rhys had instructed her to do while he rummaged in the refrigerator.

He turned, caught her eyes and smiled, his hands filled with eggs. She wondered why she'd never noticed before that his gray eyes turned almost as silver as his hair when he smiled. And she wondered if he'd resist again if she threw caution and willpower to the wind and attacked him right there in his kitchen.

Putting both hands to her temples, she tried to convince herself that it was only her hangover prompting such crazy impulses. And then she tried to believe it.

7

RHYS HAD BEEN RIGHT. Angie wasn't really going to be sick from eating. She only thought so for the first bite or two. After that, matters improved enough that she almost enjoyed the breakfast he'd prepared for her as she'd watched, fascinated.

"Feel better?" he asked when she'd finished half the meal.

"Yes, thank you. Though I still feel like a real idiot about last night," she confessed without meeting his eyes. "I haven't fallen for a stunt like that since high school."

"If it makes you feel any better, I don't think those three will play a trick like that again," he told her grimly.

She looked up quickly. "You didn't—did you fire them?"

His expression was unreadable. "Did you want me to?"

"I—" She was furious with them, true, but to cause them to lose their jobs? "No, of course not."

He nodded as if in approval of her decision. "I didn't. But I told them what I thought of their actions and informed them that I expect my staff to be mature and professional at all corporate functions, business or social. I think they got my point."

"They probably had to go change their pants," Angie murmured, toying with a half slice of toast as she pictured the scene.

"Why, Ms. St. Clair, how crude." A thread of laughter ran through his deep voice.

She looked up, realizing she'd slipped into her old habit of saying whatever she happened to be thinking. "Yes, it was, wasn't it?"

He nodded toward the glass of orange juice in front of her. "Drink your juice."

Barely resisting the urge to roll her eyes, she picked up the glass. "Yes, sir."

His eyebrows drew sharply downward. "Don't start that again, dammit."

Startled by his vehemence, she lowered the glass from her lips. "I was only teasing, Rhys."

"Oh." For a moment he looked almost sheepish. She found the expression hopelessly endearing. He studied her gravely for a moment, then reached over the table to brush his thumb across her lower lip. "Orange pulp," he explained when she caught her breath.

"Oh. I—uh—thanks." Ducking her head so that her untamed curls fell forward to conceal her flaming cheeks, she pretended to concentrate on the remainder of her meal, even though her lip was tingling like crazy. As was the rest of her.

The moment she finished eating, Angie stood and began to clear the table. "Thanks again for the first aid, Rhys," she chattered as she worked. "I owe you one. Two, actually. One for the rescue last night."

"You didn't really need rescuing, you know," he murmured, eyes never leaving her. "You were handling yourself well enough. You should be relieved to know that you aren't really an easy blonde when you've had too much to drink."

Only with you, Angie thought, cheeks flaming again as she remembered the whispered plea for him to kiss her. *But then, I don't have to be drunk to have no willpower against you, do I, Rhys?* "I don't suppose you know where my purse is," she said, hoping her even tone hid the uncomfortable clarity of her memory.

"On the dresser in my bedroom."

"I'll go get it. I'll call a cab from the phone in there." She headed for the door even as she spoke.

He followed, of course. "You won't call a cab. When you're ready to leave, I'll drive you."

She didn't bother arguing. He'd spoken in a tone she knew all too well.

She hadn't realized quite how closely he'd followed her until her hasty turn after retrieving her purse brought her right up against his chest.

He steadied her with his hands on her forearms, looming over her without making an effort to step back. "You okay?" he asked in a distracted murmur, his glittering gray eyes on her still-tingling mouth.

No, I'm not okay. I want you to kiss me again. I want you to...

"Oh, Rhys," she whispered, her shoulders sagging as she looked up at him in mute surrender.

The two kisses they'd shared thus far had been hot, rough, almost savagely hurried. This one was slow, lingering, infinitely seductive. Angie melted into his arms, purse falling unnoticed to their feet. Her arms went up, fingertips burrowing into his silver hair as he lifted her so high against his chest that her toes barely touched the floor. His tongue stabbed deep into her welcoming mouth, curling with hers, making her quiver with desires she could no longer control.

This time he'd gotten beyond her defenses and she

could think of nothing but how very much she needed to be loved by him.

"Angelique," Rhys muttered, pulling her even closer. Had he ever wanted another woman this badly? Had he ever craved another woman's touch, burned with a hunger so ravenous it threatened to consume him? Had he ever trembled for any woman before this one?

No, his mind assured him even as he lowered her to the temptingly close bed. *Never before.*

Her hand curled at the back of his head, pulling him down to her. "Dammit, Rhys," she complained just before she pressed her mouth to his.

His chuckle was strangled somewhere in the depths of that next long, thorough kiss. He knew how she felt.

Removing her dress had been torture the night before, when he'd known the treasures he'd uncovered would be denied him. It was sweet torture now, knowing how close he was to possessing those treasures. He thought fleetingly of the long months of celibacy, of fantasies concerning her—and he hoped to hell he'd be able to control himself long enough to get her clothes off.

Angie arched her back to assist him in pulling off her clothing, as impatient as he for them to be gone. Through heavy, slitted lashes she watched him as he stripped away his own shirt, slacks and briefs. Such a beautiful body, she thought raptly, avid eyes examining every perfect inch of him. Her gaze rose to his face when he leaned over her. Had she ever thought his gray eyes cold? They were flaming now, glinting with a passion she'd once thought foreign to him. His silver hair was sexily rumpled, his jaw taut with the control he tried so desperately to exert over himself. Dark splotches of color burned high on his lean cheeks. His lips—those oh-so-clever lips—were slightly parted to expose the edges of his gritted teeth. "Such a beautiful man," she murmured, raising her hands to stroke those warm, lean cheeks.

He groaned raggedly. "*You're* beautiful, so very damned beautiful." And he lowered his mouth to hers again, his fingers pushing into her tangled curls to cup her head. She was stunned to feel the unsteadiness of those fingers. Vulnerability was so incredibly seductive when it appeared in Rhys.

So this is what it's like, she thought wonderingly, arms cradling him to her aching breasts. *This is what it's like to care.*

Is this what it's like? Rhys wondered at the same time, forcing himself to ease the kiss before her tender mouth was bruised. *Is this what it's like to feel cared for?* He knew he'd never felt so thoroughly wanted.

Her throat was long, soft, pulsing. He stroked it with his lips, nibbled at the taut slope of it. Her nearly soundless moan vibrated against his mouth. He loved the feeling.

Her right shoulder curved delicately. He found a tiny round mole in the hollow and touched it with the tip of his tongue. She trembled. So did he.

Her breasts were swollen, hard tipped, glistening in the overhead light. He paused to look at them before tasting and had the satisfaction of watching the rosy tips tighten further from nothing more than the touch of his eyes. She growled her impatience and arched upward.

He closed his mouth over her, his cheeks contracting as he pulled her deep inside. She shuddered and cried out, her long, smooth legs moving restlessly against his longer, rougher ones. He threw his knee across her thighs to hold her still as he caressed her. Her fingers tightened convulsively in his hair, the tugging sensation increasing his overall hypersensitivity. He quickly reined in his galloping senses, determined to give her all the pleasure he knew how to deliver. For the first time in his empty, loveless life he cared more about a woman's pleasure than his own, and his attention to her brought him more fulfillment that he'd ever known before.

Long moments later her breasts were flushed and damp, heaving with the sobbing breaths rasping in her throat. "Please, Rhys. Oh, *please*."

Could she possibly be as hungry as he? Could she possibly need to have him inside her as desperately as he needed to be there? He fumbled in the drawer of the bedside table, his fingers closing around one of the small square packets that had been stored there so long, unneeded. He didn't have to ask whether the protection was needed now. He knew full well that it had been at least as long since Angie had made love as it had been for him.

Moments later he surged upward, taking her mouth again, fitting himself between her thighs. He paused then, anxiously aware of her small size and his own painfully substantial arousal. His fingers tested her, finding her tight, moist and so very hot, nearly sending him straight out of his mind. She pushed herself into his hand, straining for the completion that hovered just out of her reach.

"Now, Rhys. *Now*."

The husky demand shattered the last of his restraint. His hips flexed and he pressed into her, filling her until he could bury himself no more deeply. Only then did he pause, wishing dazedly that he could stop time, make this moment last indefinitely. Soft, strong arms held him tightly, and for the first time ever, he found a place where he felt as if he belonged.

But nature would not be denied. The ancient rhythm overtook him, sweeping him along toward the inevitable conclusion. He fought it, teeth grinding as he tried to postpone the culmination, that necessary end to the intimacy he'd sought for so long. But then Angie stiffened beneath him and sobbed out his name, her body convulsing around him, and he knew the limits had been reached. His harsh cry held as much protest as exultation, his body bowing into an explosive, mind-clouding climax.

He buried his face in her throat and tried to pretend that he'd never have to pull away from her.

SHE DIDN'T TRY to convince herself that she'd been wise to make love with Rhys. But she had no regrets—how could she possibly regret *that*?

Stirring reluctantly beneath him, she pushed gently at his damp shoulders. "I can't breathe," she said regretfully.

Murmuring an apology, he rolled off her, their bodies separating as he pulled her into the curve of his arm. "Better?"

She nodded against his shoulder. "Mmm-hmm."

"Are you sorry?"

"No."

She felt his muscles relax infinitesimally beneath her cheek. "Good."

She lifted her head to look at him. His eyes met hers. Why had she thought it would be any easier to read his expression now that they'd made love? His thoughts were still hidden from her. "I'm still worried about having an affair with my boss," she told him frankly. "It's not at all a prudent situation."

He frowned. "What just happened was no boss-employee fling," he told her flatly. "That was something—something neither of us had any chance of controlling," he explained with an uncharacteristic groping for words.

Propping herself on one elbow, she touched the furrow between his dark, peppered brows. "Do you know when you frown like that the skin here forms a little upside-down V?" she asked whimsically, reveling in the freedom to touch him as she chose. As she'd wanted to touch him for so very long.

He caught her hand and kissed it, then turned it within his fingers as if studying it.

"What are you thinking?" she asked softly, intrigued by his expression.

"Such a tiny hand," he murmured, his own closing fully around it. "You're so small. And so damned young. And yet you have the power to bring me to my knees. I wonder if you're aware of that."

Her eyes closed in a brief spasm. "I suppose I should know by now not to ask you a question unless I'm prepared for an honest answer," she managed, the words rather strangled.

"That's right. You should."

"I don't want to bring you to your knees, Rhys," she said in little more than a whisper. "I'm not sure anyone could do that. You're so very strong. So self-sufficient."

"Except where you're concerned," he agreed.

She dropped her cheek back to his shoulder. "What now?" she couldn't help asking.

"I don't know," he replied, his voice a deep rumble

from low in his chest. "I've got a lousy track record with relationships, Angelique. I don't want to make any promises I'm not sure I can keep."

"I'm not asking for promises," she returned promptly. "I don't even want them." Not yet. Not until she knew whether he'd still be tempted to make them once he knew the ugly truth about her father.

"If it means anything to you, I feel more for you than I've ever felt for any other woman. What just happened between us was the most incredible thing I've ever experienced."

"It means something to me," she whispered, almost unbearably touched. Her eyes felt hot, tear-laden as she lifted her face to kiss him. "It means a great deal to me."

His hand burrowed into the hair at her nape. "I want you again," he muttered against her lips. "I need you, Angelique."

Passion that had been so thoroughly sated ignited again at his hoarse words. *Rhys needed her.* For now, at least. "Yes, please, Rhys. Love me again."

RHYS WANDERED curiously around Angie's house, studying the porcelain figurines, the doilies, the crocheted afghans, the profusion of photographs and memories. "This place reminds me a little of Aunt Iris's house," he said at length. "She has things like these everywhere to remind her of the various foster kids she took in over the years."

Angie had been watching him quietly, thinking with a pang that Rhys seemed so hungry for ties—any kind of ties. Her own childhood hadn't been ideal, but at least she'd had a family, had people who'd cared for her. Rhys had had no one except a foster mother who'd been assigned him by chance—and much too late in his youth to give him the security he'd so craved. *She* could love him, she realized abruptly. She could love him exactly as he needed to be loved. But she couldn't allow herself to want too much yet. Not until she'd told him everything.

He stood in front of the piano, smiling at the grouping of photographs of Angie in various stages of growing up. "Only grandchild?" he hazarded, holding a five-by-seven print of a smiling little girl with enormous violet eyes, a blond braid and two missing teeth.

"Obviously." She took the photo out of his hands and replaced it on the piano, wondering if there were any childhood photographs of Rhys. Had anyone cared enough to have them taken? "Do you remember your mother, Rhys?"

His expression went from amused to impassive. "Not...really," he answered hesitantly. "Sometimes I have flashes—but I'm not sure how valid they are."

She rested her hand on his arm. "Tell me about them."

His shoulder shrugged, pulling at the iron-hard muscles beneath her palm. "I think I remember her laughing. Maybe singing. And I remember..." His voice trailed off, his eyes focused somewhere far in the past.

"What?"

"Waking up in the night," he answered very quietly. "Wandering through dark rooms, calling my mother. Finding her bed empty. Crawling into it and curling under the covers, knowing I was alone."

Angie was appalled. "She left you alone at night?"

His manner became more brusque. "I think so. As I said, I'm not sure how trustworthy those thirty-seven-year-old flashes may be. And since my mother was never located, there's no way to confirm them."

"Do you remember her leaving you at the hospital?"

He shook his head. "No. I think maybe I blocked that particular memory out sometime over the years. I was told that I had nightmares for several years afterward, but I don't really remember them, either. I believe they were quite—annoying to the people who raised me."

"Oh, Rhys." She buried her face in his shoulder, unable to hold back the tears.

His hand tugged at the back of her head, bringing her face up to his. One blunt, strong finger traced the salty path down her damp cheek. "Don't cry for me, Angelique. It was a long time ago."

"I'm not crying for you," she whispered, raising a hand to his cheek. "Not for the strong, successful, honorable man you've become. But I can't help crying for a frightened, lonely little boy."

The boy had grown up, but the man still craved love, whether he was aware of it or not. He needed so much, and she had so little to offer him. A soiled family reputation, a shallow, pleasure-seeking past in which she'd been too spoiled and self-centered to notice what had been going on right before her eyes. Yes, she was making her own way now, beginning to sort out her values, but would Rhys be able to trust that she'd really changed if he knew the truth? Would he think she was chasing him only because his money could reinstate her into the social circles from which she'd been ousted? Would a man who'd so relentlessly pursued respect, admiration and success be able to swallow the embarrassment of having a father-in-law in prison?

Her eyes widened at the thought, and she buried her face in his shoulder again to hide her expression. Marriage? How could she possibly think of marriage? Had she—oh, yes, she *had*. She'd fallen in love with Rhys Wakefield. And on top of all her other doubts about becoming involved with him, she wondered if a man who had never known love could ever learn to share it.

Holding her small, sweetly curved body tightly in his arms, Rhys rested his cheek on her silky blond head. She held herself closely against him, but for some reason he had the feeling that she'd pulled back emotionally. Was his past so distasteful to her that she didn't think she could deal with it? Would she not allow herself to become too deeply involved with anyone whose childhood was so dramatically different from her own moneyed, privileged one? What *was* she thinking? he wondered in frustration.

She was going to break his heart, he thought bleakly. He'd never really understood that particular, rather dramatic phrase. Now he did. And wished he didn't.

He could almost feel her gathering her emotions and placing them under tight restraint. And then she pulled away, her expression carefully shuttered, her smile bright and meaningless. "Would you like some lunch?" she asked, automatically smoothing her hair. "Just let me change into fresh clothes and I'll—"

Something snapped in his head, manifesting itself in a surge of temper. He caught her roughly in his arms. "Don't do that, dammit! Not to me."

Her eyes widened in obvious surprise as she braced herself against his chest with splayed hands. "Don't do what?" she asked, confused.

"Don't give me polite little social smiles and speak to me as though I'm someone with whom you have to make pleasant conversation. If you've got something you want to say to me, say it." *Tell me it's over*, he challenged her with his eyes. *Tell me you don't want me. I dare you.*

But she never reacted exactly as he expected. Her startled expression slowly changed, becoming delightfully willful. "Kiss me, Rhys."

She made him crazy when she tilted her little chin to that imperious angle. As if she were daring him to do something about it. It was a dare he couldn't resist. He crushed her mouth beneath his, his body leaping into heated response. He was pleased to note that her eyes were glazed when he finally lifted his head, though he ruefully suspected his own held the same look. "Now what?" he grated.

"Now make love to me," she ordered, her hands sliding boldly up his chest.

"*That's* the way I like to hear you talk," he approved with a choked laugh. And for the third time he yanked down the zipper of the now-rather-crumpled pastel dress. He left it lying in a careless heap on the floor when he lifted her into his arms and carried her to bed.

IT WAS LATE in the afternoon when they finally got around to eating lunch. Rhys played with her cat while Angie stirred together a chicken salad and hollowed out tomatoes for stuffing. He refused to call the cat "Flower," declaring that to be the dumbest name for an animal he'd ever heard. Sitting Indian-style on the floor of the kitchen, he wiggled his fingers enticingly in front of the crouching half-grown kitten. "Pounce on it, cat. I dare you."

"Ouch!" he muttered a moment later when several sharp little claws sank into his forefinger. Shaking the cat off his hand, he examined the two tiny drops of scarlet at his knuckle. "Damn."

Angie laughed at him, setting their lunch on the table. Dressed now in jeans and a red cotton sweater, she was amazingly comfortable with him, not even tempted to slip into the coolly professional mode she'd tried so hard to maintain around him at the beginning. It was rather hard to act dignified when she'd just rolled all over her bed with him, she thought wryly, even as she said, "You shouldn't have dared her. She doesn't know she's supposed to be intimidated by the mighty Rhys Wakefield."

"She's got a lot in common with her owner," Rhys murmured, pushing himself to his feet.

"Want to register any complaints?"

Washing his hands at the kitchen sink, he shot her a look over his shoulder. "Not at the moment."

"Good. Then I'll let you sit at my table."

"How gracious of you."

She sank her fork into her chicken-stuffed tomato. "I thought so."

He was grinning when he picked up his own fork. Angie eyed that grin through her lashes, pleased that he looked so relaxed. He needed to play more often, she decided. She'd make sure that he did—for as long as she had the opportunity to do so.

Rhys seemed in no hurry to leave after lunch, nor was Angie anxious for him to do so. He acted a bit startled when she suggested a word game, but agreed to try it.

"You've never played this?" she asked, setting the playing pieces on the coffee table as they settled on the floor on either side of it.

"No."

"We try to make words at the same time from the

same letter cubes.'' She explained the rules, then shook the cubes. ''Ready?''

He nodded. ''Why not?''

She couldn't remember laughing so much in a long time. Not during the past year, anyway. Rhys approached game playing in the same grim, single-minded manner he ran a business. The words he found in the arrangement of cubes were neatly written on his pad, most of them four-or five-letter words. Her own lists were hastily scribbled, mostly three-letter words—some of them made-up, which *really* confused him. ''Gup?'' he repeated, giving her a quizzical frown.

''I don't suppose you'd believe it's a baby guppy?''

''We could get the dictionary,'' he suggested.

She laughed, shaking her head. ''Oh, for heaven's sake, Rhys, there's no such word. I was just being silly.''

''Oh. Well, you can still have the points if you want them,'' he offered magnanimously.

The needlepoint throw pillow missed his head by inches. ''*Now* what'd I say?'' he demanded, hands on his hips as he looked at her in exasperation, causing her to go off in another peal of giggles.

''Really, Rhys, don't you ever—''

But Rhys was distracted by a rattling noise from the vicinity of the front door, making it useless for her to finish the question. ''What was that?'' he demanded.

''The mailman,'' she answered, rising and headed toward the door. ''What did you think it was—a prowler? In the middle of the afternoon?''

He grunted. Angie wondered if men were born with the ability to express so much with one nonverbal sound or if it was a trait they picked up from other men.

A glance through her mail effectively erased her smile. Along with the assortment of bills and letters-to-occupant was an envelope bearing the return address of the prison where her father was currently residing. She stood very still, looking at it for a long time.

Why was he writing her? Hadn't they said everything they'd needed to say the last time they'd seen each other? She'd told him exactly what she thought of his business practices and shady ethics, to which he'd retorted that she'd never seemed to care where his money came from as long as she had a closet full of designer clothes and a fancy new sportscar in which to attend her many social functions. That had stung. Mostly because it had been so true.

"What's wrong?" Rhys demanded, proving she hadn't guarded her expression quite as well as she'd hoped. "Has something upset you?"

She cleared her face for a smile. "No, of course not. Just a stack of bills. No one ever enjoys receiving them." Placing the bills on the small desk at one side of the room, she tossed the letter from her father into the wastebasket at its side, unopened. She wasn't interested in anything he had to say. She noticed that Rhys looked at the wastebasket for a moment, but she was relieved when he didn't comment. "Did you want to play another game?" he asked instead.

She tilted her head and looked at him. Sitting on the floor, his shirt haphazardly buttoned only halfway up his chest, his slacks stretched across his spread thighs, his gorgeous hair reflecting the overhead light, he looked too good to be real. It was hard to believe she could go up to this man and run her hands all over that body, if she so desired. A rather smug smile tilting her lips, she decided abruptly that she *did* so desire.

The smile blossoming into a full-fledged grin, she launched herself at him, taking him by surprise and causing him to tumble backward onto the worn rag rug. "I just thought of another game I'd rather play," she informed him, shackling his wrists in her small hands at either side of his head.

His eyes lighting with startled pleasure, he smiled. "Be my guest," he invited her.

"Oh, but you have to cooperate or it won't be any fun," she informed him.

"You'll have to teach me the rules," he challenged, lying very still beneath her.

Straddling him, his wrists still shackled within her hands, she lowered her head to nibble at the firm line of his jaw. "I can handle that."

His eyes narrowed to sexy, dark slits. "I think you can handle just about anything, Boston."

Some of her humor dimming, she wondered if she could possibly begin to handle Rhys. He seemed to have more confidence in her than she did. Shoving her doubts to the back of her mind, she concentrated on the man lying so temptingly beneath her. "I thought of a name for this new game," she murmured before running the tip of her tongue around the nicely molded shell of his ear.

"What's that?" His voice had gotten decidedly hoarse, she noted in satisfaction, wondering how long he'd be content to lie still and allow her to take control of the lovemaking. There was a heady sense of power in having the upper hand for once with the masterful Rhys Wakefield.

"I think I'll call it 'Drive the Man Insane.'" She squirmed sinuously against him, her breasts rubbing slowly against his chest.

"You've been doing that from the moment you walked into my office," he grated, his hips shifting restlessly against the carpet.

She dragged her lips across his cheek to his mouth. There she nibbled, teased, kissed until his lips strained upward, silently inviting her to deepen the embraces. The very tip of her tongue traced his lips. He had a wonderful mouth, she thought, already losing herself in the heated oblivion of desire. Rhys's hands quivered in hers. She sensed his rising impatience even as she became aware that he had grown very hard beneath her.

Being wanted so obviously by Rhys made her even more bold. Motioning for him to lie still, she sat up and began to unbutton his shirt, her eyes locked with his. She ran her hands lingeringly down his sleek chest, pausing to draw decreasing circles around his erect nipples, tracing his rib cage as it expanded and contracted with his increasingly ragged breathing. Leaning over again, she planted moist, openmouthed kisses down the center of his chest, scooting lower until her lips were pressed to the smooth skin of his stomach. And then she unfastened his jeans.

Taking a deep breath, she slipped a hand inside the opening and stroked him, loving the hot, solid, throbbing feel of him. He groaned softly, hips arching in an unconscious rhythm. "You're killing me, Boston," he managed roughly.

"I've only just begun, Rhys," she whispered in sultry promise. And then she lowered her mouth to him.

Rhys stiffened as if electrified. He moaned his pleasure with the direction her "game" had taken. And he lasted only moments before abandoning his acquiescent role. Muttering her name, he rolled her to her back, looming over her as his mouth covered hers. His hands were already busy, stripping her out of her sweater and jeans.

Arching into his hands, Angie gave herself up to his lead. She'd enjoyed being in charge while it had lasted, she decided with one of her last coherent thoughts. She'd have to try it again sometime. Sometime very soon.

8

"SO ARE YOU GOING to marry the woman or what?"

Rhys held the receiver a few inches away and stared at it, startled by the blunt question that had immediately followed his answering the phone. He brought it carefully back to his ear. "Graham?"

"Well, of course it's Graham. Who the hell did you think it was? Answer my question."

"I—uh—what woman?" Rhys asked inanely.

Graham's snort of response was noisy and quite expressive. "What woman, he asks," he grumbled. "I find a beautiful blonde in his office, nearly get my head taken off at the shoulders for daring to ask her to dinner and he wants to know what woman. The man's elevator stops somewhere short of the penthouse."

Rhys looked heavenward, the wry expression going unappreciated since he happened to be alone at the moment. "Graham, did you ruin the peace of my Sunday afternoon at home because you wanted to talk to me or to mutter insults about me?"

"I called to ask you a question—one you still haven't answered, I might point out. Are you going to marry her? And if you ask who, I'm going to do something violent."

"That won't be necessary. I know who you're talking about," Rhys said with a sigh of resignation. "Angelique."

"So...?"

"The subject hasn't come up."

"You mean it hasn't occurred to you, or you haven't gotten around to asking her yet?"

"I don't suppose it would do any good for me to point out that this is none of your business?"

"Has it ever done any good in the past?"

"No," Rhys admitted.

"Right. So...?"

Rhys dropped into a chair and leaned back, his long, denim-covered legs stretched in front of him, his eyes focused bleakly on his soft leather moccasins. "I'm not going to marry her."

"Why the hell not?" Graham bellowed, making Rhys wince and hold the receiver a bit further from his ear.

"Several reasons. Chief among them that I sincerely doubt the lady would be interested."

"And just why might that be? She's interested in you now, isn't she?"

Rhys thought of the past weekend. He'd left Angie that morning only because he'd desperately needed a couple of hours of rest and knew he wouldn't get them as long as she was in the same house with him. Judging from the dazed look in her purple-shadowed eyes, she had been in much the same condition. He'd driven straight home, never even considering a stop by the office, taken a quick shower and fallen into bed for three hours of deep, undisturbed sleep. He'd be worried about getting old if it wasn't for the fact that he hadn't made love that many times in that few hours even at the height of his sexual experimentation in his late teens.

"She's interested at the moment," he conceded.

"And what makes you think it won't last?"

"Come on, Graham, you saw her. She's young, beautiful, intelligent."

"And you're Quasimodo."

Rhys ignored that. "I'm fourteen years older."

"And you've got the body of a thirty-year-old and the mind of a twelve-year-old. So what?"

He couldn't quite swallow the chuckle. "Dammit, Graham."

"Fine. You don't want her—*I'll* marry her. I'm a year younger than you and infinitely more attractive. She'll be taking a major step up."

Rhys stately clearly and crudely what his former best friend could do with himself once the call was concluded.

"Well, stop being such an humble jackass, Wakefield. It would have been obvious to a blind man that you're head over heels in love with the woman. And she was equally dazzled by you for some incomprehensible reason. So instead of taking advantage of the best thing that's happened to you in years by marrying her immediately, what do you do? You sit around and whine that you're not good enough for her. 'sdisgusting."

"You're paying me back, right? For telling you that Michaelson woman was only after your money. Just because it turned out I was right, you've never really forgiven me."

"Of course I forgave you. You saved me from a fate worse than death. But it also set a precedent for well-intentioned interference. So I'm following suit. You're the best friend I've ever had, Rhys—and don't expect me to ever repeat that, because I'm quite sure one or both of us would puke if I did. But anyway, if ever I've seen a man more in need of a wife and kids than you, I didn't know it at the time."

"So how come you've never taken your own advice?" Rhys demanded, resisting the urge to challenge that statement, which he knew would only lead to a lengthy, fruitless argument.

"Hey, I've been looking for a woman with the face of an angel, the voice of a musical instrument and the eyes of an innocent temptress. I'm thoroughly hacked off that you found her first."

Rhys couldn't help smiling at the flowery description. Angelique would hate it. He couldn't help agreeing with it. "I wouldn't know what to do with a wife and kids if someone gave them to me."

"You'd love 'em, Rhys," Graham answered, his gruff voice suddenly serious. "With the same single-minded devotion you give that blasted company of yours. And they'd be damned lucky. Give it some thought. I gotta go. Talk to you later."

"Graham, wait, I—" Rhys exhaled in frustration when he found himself talking to a dial tone. His head ached dully when he recradled the receiver. It wasn't an uncommon reaction to one of Graham's whirlwind conversations.

The call left him restless and slightly bemused. He roamed aimlessly around his house for half an hour, noting for the first time that it could use more furniture. He'd only lived there for four or five years, so he really hadn't paid much attention before. He'd bought it because he hated apartment living—all those people under the same roof with him. When he'd moved in, he'd brought with him the furniture he'd already accumulated. He wondered if Angelique would be interested in helping him fix the place up a bit.

He thought about going to the office, but the idea didn't appeal to him at the moment. There was nothing really pressing for him to do there, so he'd be just as bored and just as fidgety. He thought again of Angelique, and his body immediately responded with a renewed surge of energy, causing him to shake his head in wonder. The woman was dangerous, he decided. And because his reactions to her made him nervous, he made no effort to call her. He needed time to get himself under control before seeing her at work the next morning, he thought grimly.

He didn't know what impulse made him pick up the phone and dial Aunt Iris's number.

The aging woman's voice sounded weaker than it had the last time he'd talked to her—less than a week before. "How are you?" he asked, concern making his tone more brusque than usual.

Knowing him so well, his former foster mother wasn't intimidated by that tone. "I'm doing just fine, dear. How are *you*?"

"I'm okay."

"You're working too hard, you're not eating right and you're not getting enough rest," she translated, a smile in her quavery voice.

His own smile was a tender one. "Something like that."

"I got the check you sent me yesterday. You really must stop being so extravagant, Rhys. You know I have my social security. You work hard for your money. You should—"

"Spend it any way I dam—darned well please," he amended quickly. "And it pleases me to send some of it to you. Tell Polly to get you those chocolates you like.

And a pretty new bed jacket to wear for me when I visit you next month."

"She's already bought me the chocolates," Aunt Iris admitted cheerfully. "I've been into them this morning. They're better than ever."

"I'm glad you're enjoying them. Polly's taking good care of you, then?"

"Yes, she's a lovely girl. And she should be taking good care of me with the generous salary you're paying her. You're too good to me, Rhys."

"You're the best thing that ever happened to me," he replied gruffly. "I owe you a lot more than money. And, besides, I've got too much just for myself, anyway."

"Then get yourself a family to spoil," she returned instantly, the response a familiar one. Aunt Iris worried more than Graham about Rhys's self-imposed isolation. It bothered Rhys that she worried about him. He didn't want to be the cause of any distress for her.

Because he thought it would make her feel better—and maybe it had been the reason he'd called in the first place, if he was honest with himself—he said quietly, "I've—um—started seeing someone, Aunt Iris. You'd like her, I think."

A new note of interest entered her voice. "Tell me about her."

Rhys tried to put Angelique into words, describing her lovely appearance, her brisk competence at work, briefly touching on her unhappy recent past.

"She needs you," Iris told him with satisfaction.

"She needs someone," he corrected cautiously. "For now. That doesn't mean she'll be content to stay with me for long."

"If she has any sense at all, she will. And from what

you've told me, she's a woman with a great deal of sense. I want to meet her."

"Maybe I'll bring her with me next month," Rhys offered rashly. "If we're still seeing each other then."

"You will be. The young man I know so well won't let the first woman he's ever loved get away without a fight."

Rhys was startled. "I didn't say I was in love with her."

"You didn't have to," she answered gently, amused. "It's in your voice every time you say her name. Angelique. Such a beautiful name."

"I don't know much about this love thing, Aunt Iris. I haven't had much experience with it," Rhys confessed, finally verbalizing one of his concerns about his relationship with Angelique.

"Oh, my dear boy. You have more potential for loving than any man I've ever known. Look at the way you take such good care of me. I helped raise a lot of kids in my time as a foster mother, and though quite a few of them have stayed in touch over the years, you're the only one who makes me feel as though I truly have a son of my own. You've got so much to offer a woman and some babies. So much love dammed up inside you, just waiting to be released. I love you, Rhys, and I want you to be happy."

"I—uh—love you, too," he muttered, hoping she could hear him. He hadn't told her often enough over the years, but it was still so very hard for him to say. Was he in love with Angelique? And if so, would he ever be able to say those words to her?

"I know you do. I'm tired now, dear. It's time for my nap."

"All right. Take care of yourself. I'll talk to you in a couple of days."

"Don't let her get away, Rhys."

Murmuring something incoherent, Rhys gently disconnected the call. He wasn't sure if his talk with Aunt Iris had made anything more clear to him or not. But it had felt awfully good to talk to her. If only it hadn't left him with this nagging anxiety about her.

ANGIE HELD HER HEAD HIGH as she entered her office on Monday morning. It wasn't easy. She had the most ridiculous urge to slink in and hope she wasn't noticed.

Something in the smiling good-mornings she was given in the hallways told her that she'd been the topic of office gossip since leaving the party Friday evening. She could just hear it. Ms. St. Clair, the straitlaced, no-nonsense "deputy dictator" had gotten herself smashed at the office party, and Rhys Wakefield, who'd never before gone out of his way on behalf of anyone to their knowledge, had yelled at the men responsible and then taken her home. Fully half the other employees had probably suspected then that she and Rhys were having an affair. At the time, they'd have been wrong. Now, they were absolutely right. She gulped.

Or *were* they having an affair? Did one day and one night of incredible, teeth-rattling, mind-spinning, repeated lovemaking constitute an affair? Was it going to happen again? And if so, why hadn't Rhys called her last night when she'd waited up until midnight hoping he'd do so? Had he been giving her time to recuperate, or had he started to regret the involvement with his assistant, which would prove so awkward at the office?

It seemed she had a lot of questions, she thought

wryly, stowing her purse in her desk. If only she had a few answers to go with them.

She hadn't been at work for half an hour before Rhys summoned her.

"Good morning. How do you feel?" June asked solicitously when Angie passed her desk.

As if a hangover lasted three days, Angie thought with a mental sigh. "I'm fine, thanks, June."

"Well, you look wonderful. Come to think of it, Mr. Wakefield looks wonderful today, too. Very relaxed." June's voice was as smugly satisfied as if she took full credit for Rhys's state of mind.

"That's, uh—" Angie kept her eyes trained on Rhys's door, unable to finish the weak comment. Her hand wasn't quite steady when she tapped on his door. Would he greet her with the smile she'd seen and melted over during the weekend? Or would he be back to business as usual, the aberrance of the weekend put firmly behind him?

More questions, she thought, turning the doorknob. But this one was about to be answered.

Rhys looked up from his desk as she entered. "Good morning, Angelique. Where do we stand on the Phoenix project? I assume you've checked the figures?"

She wasn't quite sure *what* to make of him this morning, Angie decided as she automatically filled him in on the first thing she'd done upon entering her office. His question was completely businesslike, but his eyes, his voice and his smile were all—warm, she thought, resisting the impulse to fan herself with the steno book in her hand. Intimate. Full of memories she shared.

"Sit down and let's go over this," he instructed, nodding toward her usual chair beside his desk. "I'm not too comfortable with our rate of production on this one. What do you think?''

I think I'm in big trouble, Rhys Wakefield. Because I love you. And because I'm only a hair's breadth away from pouncing on you and begging you to make love to me right there on your desk. "I think you're right to be concerned," she said in a clear, brisk tone, sitting gracefully in the chair and crossing her legs. "The production rate is way down on this one. Why do you think that is?"

RHYS MADE IT THROUGH most of the day without losing his precarious control, and the effort exhausted him much more than the pile of work he and Angie waded through during those hours. Sitting only a few scant feet away from her, catching an occasional tantalizing whiff of her light fragrance, watching her neat mauve jacket shift over her soft breasts when she moved, surreptitiously eyeing the length of long, smooth legs that he could almost feel around his back—it was a wonder he could speak without drooling and stammering, he thought grimly.

He wasn't sure what snapped his control late in the afternoon. Maybe it was the way she'd been nibbling on a pencil as she studied a report June had typed for them. Watching her, he'd broken into a fine sweat, finding it necessary to loosen his tie. Or maybe the way she looked up with a quick laugh and a teasing remark when he made a desperate grab for his coffee cup and knocked it over, swearing as coffee spilled over the top of his desk and splashed onto his slacks.

Or maybe he was only human and could hold back his natural desires not one moment longer.

Whatever the cause, he shoved his chair away from

his desk with enough violence to cause her to look up from her renewed pencil nibbling with startled inquiry, reached out to snatch the pencil from her hand and had her in his arms, all before she could say a word. The report June had spent four hours working on fell to the floor.

It had been thirty-one hours since he'd kissed her, he'd calculated only moments before. It felt more like thirty-one days. He devoured her mouth as if he'd been starving—and maybe he had been. After one brief, shocked moment of hesitation, Angie slid her arms around his neck and kissed him back as if she'd been every bit as hungry.

He pulled away only to draw a quick, impatient breath. "Again," he muttered, holding her closer.

"What if—?"

He didn't give her the chance to finish the question. He knew she'd been about to express a concern that someone would walk in. That was unlikely and they both knew it. No one except Graham dared to enter Rhys's office without knocking first. Not even Angie. So he continued to kiss her without thought of anything except how very right she felt in his arms, how much he'd missed her since having her there last.

Long moments later, he slowly, reluctantly drew back. Much more of that, he thought ruefully, and he'd be tempted to test the privacy of his office even more daringly.

Angie looked rather dazed. He smiled and touched a finger to her warm, flushed cheek. "Thanks," he said with a lightness at odds with the roughness of his voice, "I needed that."

"I—um—wasn't expecting that," she told him unnecessarily, her own voice not quite normal.

"You should have been. It was all I could do not to go for you hours ago."

Her color deepened. She lifted a hand to her disheveled hair, then stroked her little finger over her smudged lips. "I must look as though I've just been thoroughly kissed," she scolded.

"At least you don't look as though you've just been thoroughly—"

"Rhys!"

He chuckled at her shocked exclamation. "Have dinner with me tonight?"

She moistened her lips, and Rhys fought the urge to pull her back into his arms. "In a restaurant?" she asked hesitantly.

He gave her a look. "No, in a bookstore. Where did you think?"

"What if someone from the office sees us out together? Aren't you worried about the gossip?"

"Screw the gossip," he answered inelegantly, annoyed by her implication that he wanted to hide their relationship. Hell, he wouldn't care if the whole world saw her on his arm, knew she belonged to him—for the moment, anyway, he amended quickly, warning himself not to start wanting too much. He'd learned early in life that wanting and getting were usually two very different things. "Do you want to have dinner with me or not?"

"Yes, Rhys," she answered gently, touching his cheek with her fingertips. "I'd love to have dinner with you.'"

He caught her hand in his, trying not to crush it. "Then go home and change," he said rather hoarsely. "I'll pick you up at seven."

She glanced in surprise at her watch. It was just past five. "You want me to leave now?"

"Unless you want to test the possibilities of that leather couch," he answered bluntly.

Her eyes widened. And then she smiled. "Tempting as that is, I think I'll take you up on your advice to go home and change."

"Maybe that would be best," he agreed. He watched her cross the office, toss a smile over her shoulder and walk out the door. And then he exhaled in a gust of frustration and ripped off his already loosened tie.

HE HAD GOOD INTENTIONS to take her to a very nice restaurant to prove to her that he was proud to be seen with her. He really did. He'd even managed to make reservations on short notice. But the moment she opened her door, looking cool and stunning in her simply cut black dress and sexy high-heeled sandals, all he could think about was throwing her over his shoulder and hauling her off to bed.

"Angelique. You look so damned beautiful."

She started to thank him, then noted the hungry, almost savage look on his face. He smiled and tossed her purse onto a table. And then she held out her hands to him. "We can eat later," she assured him gently.

He groaned and caught her in his arms. "Yeah," he murmured distractedly, his hands already caressing her back through the clingy, silky black fabric. "Later."

MUCH LATER, Rhys groaned again—apologetically, this time. "Are you mad?" he asked tentatively.

With some effort, she lifted her head from his shoulder. "Why should I be mad?" she asked, honestly confused. How could she be mad after Rhys had made such beautiful, sensitive, glorious love to her?

"I promised to take you out to dinner. I suppose it's too late now."

She smiled at his sheepish look. "I suppose so," she replied without undue concern. "We'll have to find something here. I'm sure we can make do."

He frowned at her teasing smile. "I'm *not* afraid to be seen in public with you," he informed her flatly. "It's just that I—uh—"

"Took one look at me and got carried away with passion," she finished for him, feeling decidedly smug.

His mouth quirked. "Yeah. Something like that."

She reached up to kiss him lightly. "Now how could I possibly be mad about that?"

He hugged her, and the gesture was so natural, so sweet and unexpectedly romantic that she had to blink back tears. And then he spoke. "You're a good sport, Boston."

A good sport? So much for romance, she thought wryly, suppressing a sigh as the incipient tears evaporated. "What would you like to eat?" she asked, reaching for her robe.

Fifteen minutes later she stood at the stove, pressing a spatula against two sizzling hamburgers as Rhys prepared buns and condiments. The black dress having seemed inappropriate for such an informal dinner at home, she'd wrapped herself in a pink terry robe. Rhys wore the slacks to his suit, his unbuttoned shirt flapping over them, sleeves rolled up to his elbows. He looked so good that she had to force herself to concentrate on the burgers. "How do you want yours?"

"Rare."

"Of course." Now why hadn't she guessed? Smiling

to herself, she slipped his undercooked patty onto one
of the buns he had ready, prepared to let hers cook a
while longer.

"Tomorrow night we'll eat out," Rhys promised,
carrying his plate to the table. "We'll leave straight
from the office so we don't risk getting distracted
again."

He seemed to be taking for granted that they'd be
spending a great deal of their spare time together. Angie had no complaints, but she wondered how long it
would last. She had a nagging suspicion that the more
time she spent with Rhys, the harder it would be when
he grew tired of the affair. "All right."

He gave her a quick glance, as if something in her
voice puzzled him, but didn't comment.

They talked casually over dinner. Rhys slipped
pieces of meat to her hovering cat and Angie pretended not to notice as they touched on politics, relig-
ion, current events—anything but work. The conversation eventually came around to Aunt Iris. "I talked to
her yesterday," he commented, swirling the ice in his
soda.

"How is she?"

"She sounds weaker all the time. Her health has
been going downhill for the past couple of years."

Angie covered his restless hand with hers. "You
must be quite worried about her," she said with ready
sympathy.

He nodded. "Yeah. I am."

"Maybe you should go see her," she suggested carefully.

"I'm going next month. I told her about you."

She looked startled but not displeased, he noted,
eyeing her through his lashes.

"Did you?"

"Yeah. She'd like to meet you. I told her maybe you'd come with me when I visit."

She pulled her hand back to her lap, looking searchingly at him. "Why, Rhys?" she asked in little more than a whisper.

"Because it's—important to me," he answered hesitantly. "I'd like for you to meet her."

"I'd love to meet her, if you really want me to."

There were so many things he wanted to say to her. And, paradoxically, so little he could actually think of to say. The cat meowed plaintively at his feet, and he fed it the last bite of his burger. "I want you to," he said without looking up from the greedy kitten.

"Tell me more about her," she urged, pushing her plate away and leaning encouragingly against the table.

He found himself talking more about himself than he had in years. About a rootless, angry teenager who'd had too many disappointments, too little security. Who'd been hugged so rarely that he instinctively mistrusted the woman who'd taken him in with open arms and a welcoming smile. About the time she'd chewed him out so fiercely for trying to take money from her, and about the time she'd spent part of the little extra money she had to buy him an expensive jacket because all the other boys in his class were wearing them. About the hours she'd spent standing over him, making sure he did his homework, and the tears she'd shed when the service had called and he'd struck out on his own to face dangers she dreaded for him. About the years of occasional visits and telephone calls, cards and letters, her reluctance to take his money and his pleasure that she'd finally accepted his need to offer it.

"You love her," Angie concluded softly when he finally stopped talking with an uncomfortable flush of embarrassment at going on for so long.

"I love her," he agreed in a mutter, shifting in his chair. "She's the closest thing to family I ever remember having."

"I can't wait to meet her. She must be very special."

"She is. You'll like her." *You're a lot like her*, he mused silently. *Special*.

"I'm sure I will."

"What's your own family like, Angelique?" Rhys asked with an effort at nonchalance, still unwilling to reveal that he'd had her investigated. He wanted very badly for her to share her secrets with him voluntarily.

"My mother's dead. My father and I aren't close," she answered tersely, her face deliberately emptied of all expression. She reached abruptly for the dishes. "I'll clear this away. Why don't you watch television or something and relax awhile?"

"I'll help you," he offered, standing.

"No," she said quickly, her face averted. "I'll get it. You go play with Flower. I think she's feeling a bit neglected tonight."

She'd shut him out, he realized grimly, walking slowly into the other room. At the least hint of probing into her past, she'd deliberately shut him out, despite the confidences he'd shared with her about his own. It hurt, he discovered. More than he'd expected.

The black-and-white cat purring contentedly in his lap as he stared at the dark television screen, Rhys comforted himself with the memory of her promise to visit Aunt Iris with him in a few weeks. At least she didn't seem to be in any hurry to end their relationship, though she was still unwilling to trust him completely. It seemed he was willing to settle for whatever he could get, for now.

9

RHYS TRIED NOT TO DWELL on how closely Angelique sat to him on the couch as they worked side by side in his office the next afternoon. Dammit, he thought, scowling down at the reports spread on the table in front of them, he was going to have to get his responses to her under control if he was going to continue working with her.

He almost winced as he remembered the number of times his concentration had wandered during the staff meeting earlier. At one point he'd actually found himself staring at Angelique's legs, having completely lost track of the discussion that had skidded to a halt as everyone waited for him to speak. He'd recovered by clearing his throat and muttering something about having a new idea for increasing the efficiency of the shipping department records system. No one had seemed to question his words.

He'd thought it wryly amusing that his staff considered him so dauntingly, mechanically dedicated to his business that his attention would never turn to anything else. He'd actually found himself smiling when he thought of how stunned everyone would have been had they seen their no-nonsense employer and his cool, dignified assistant rolling on the floor of her living room on Saturday afternoon. Could any of their associates begin to imagine the passion Angelique concealed behind her sleek hairstyles and tailored suits? They'd be even less likely to believe the passion she was able to bring out in him.

Noticing that his faint smile was making several of his subordinates visibly nervous, he'd immediately suppressed it and gotten back to business. And yet here he was now, ogling his assistant, business again forgotten as he fantasized about all the possibilities of a leather couch and a large desk. Would there ever come a time when he could be in the same room with her without wanting her this badly?

He turned his gaze reluctantly back to the reports. "Get the MedPak file out of the bottom drawer of my desk," he told her more curtly than he'd intended.

If the brusqueness of the command bothered her, she didn't let it show. Standing, she smoothed her skirt, drawing his eyes once more back to her gorgeous legs, and then walked over to the desk. The woman knew how to walk, Rhys thought with a mental groan.

She had the drawer open before he remembered the other file he'd shoved into it. "Angelique, wait!" he snapped, just as she opened the file she'd extracted to make sure it was the correct one.

She raised her head very slowly. The stricken look in her violet eyes made his stomach clench. She turned her gaze back down to the incriminating papers in her hands, hiding her expression. "You had me investigated." Her voice was strangled, barely audible.

Hell. He rose slowly to his feet, hands spread apologetically. "Let me explain."

She closed the folder and set it on the desk, the stricken look gone, wiped out along with all other emotion. "I'm sure I understand. As your executive assistance, I'm privy to a great deal of confidential information. It's important that you know I can be trusted. I was surprised all along that you hired me without knowing more about me." Her voice lowered, her face carefully averted from him. "I just wish you had told me, especially once we became—"

"Lovers," he supplied bluntly when her words trailed away. "And I didn't have you investigated because of the job, Angelique. It was strictly personal."

She whirled to face him, her eyes flaring now with a particularly recognizable emotion—anger. "You invaded my privacy because you were *curious*?" she demanded incredulously. "Or was I good enough to work for you when you didn't know anything about my past, but not quite good enough to sleep with until you'd found out everything? Well, how does it feel to find out that you've been to bed with the daughter of a criminal, Rhys?"

"Angelique—"

Quivering with fury he could only assume was fueled by genuine hurt, she slapped her hand down onto the desk. "You know, I actually believed you last night when you said you'd intended to take me to a public restaurant. But it wasn't office gossip you were worried about at all, was it? You didn't want this respectable reputation you've built for yourself to be endangered by the possibility of anyone recognizing Nolan St. Clair's socially outcast daughter at your—"

"That's enough!" Rhys caught her forearm in a grip that would have left bruises had he not immediately loosened it. "You know damn well I don't care who sees us together in public. That I intended to take you to that restaurant. Don't you? *Don't you?*"

She looked up at him, a hasty answer quivering on

her lips, then paused when their eyes locked. Her gaze fell first. "Yes," she admitted in a reluctant mutter.

Satisfied with that minor victory, he released her. "I had you investigated because I was worried about you," he told her grimly. "I've known for some time about your father, and I couldn't care less what he did as long as his stupidity is not still hurting you."

"You were worried about me? Why?" She searched his face anxiously, obviously trying to make sense of his unexpected confession.

Did he have to spell out everything to her? "Because you seemed so alone. Because it was obvious that something was hurting you and I wanted to know if there was anything I could do to help. Because I care about you, dammit."

Angie stared at him, chewing her lower lip as she considered his words. On one hand, she'd have found it easier to believe that he'd done what he had because of the natural concerns of an employer who must trust his assistant with so much. On the other, she'd never known Rhys to lie to her or to anyone else. If he said he'd invaded her privacy because he was concerned about her, she had no choice but to believe him.

He cared about her. She knew he was attracted to her, knew that their relationship was more than just a physical one. But she'd been very careful not to try to define it too specifically. Of course she'd known for some time that she was in love with him. But she'd never expected that love to be returned or to have a happy ending to this whirlwind affair.

No, she thought, looking away from the fire in his molten gray eyes. She couldn't put too much faith in his words. He was…infatuated, perhaps, with her now, but for how long could it last? Eventually it would start to bother him that her father was in prison, that she, herself, had been investigated for collusion. Surely he wouldn't want a woman with that type of scandal in her past as his wife, as the mother of his children.

Others had claimed to care for her. Her father—and look how deeply he'd hurt her, how badly he'd let her down. Her friends in Boston, who'd dumped her without a backward glance when it was no longer fashionable to be seen with her. Other men who'd wanted her, but had been unwilling to give what she had craved. How could she possibly put her faith in this troubled, complex man who had so much yet to learn about loving? She'd been hurt too badly. She was horribly afraid of being hurt again.

Her hands gripping her forearms as if in response to a chill, she turned away from him. "Rhys, I'd like to go home early today, if you don't mind. I need some time alone." It was the first time in the months she'd worked for him that she'd asked to leave early.

"Let me take you home," he offered immediately. "We'll spend the afternoon together. We'll talk. We need to talk, Angelique."

She couldn't suppress her slight gasp of surprise. Rhys was willing to walk away from an important project because she was upset? Was it possible that he cared more than she'd allowed herself to believe? "I really need to be alone for a while, Rhys. I'll see you in the morning, all right?"

He looked disappointed, but nodded resignedly. "All right. Call me if you change your mind about talking later, will you? It isn't always necessary to handle everything alone, you know."

She turned to make her escape before she gave in to the impulse to throw herself at him. Before she could slip through the door, she found herself whirled abruptly into his arms. "I'm sorry, Angelique," he muttered, his dark eyes boring intently into hers. "I didn't mean to hurt you. I was only trying to help."

Her heart thudded against him, her mouth going dry. Even after the emotional shocks of the past few minutes, her body still reacted to being pressed against his. "I know you were."

His kiss was gentle, tender, indescribably sweet. She could have almost called it loving. When he released her, she was trembling, and she suspected that he was, too. "Call me if you need me," he repeated huskily.

She couldn't answer. Instead, she turned and fled.

LOCKED INTO THE REFUGE of her grandmother's house, Angie sat wrapped in her soft warm robe, Flower on her lap as she stared at nothing. She'd been sitting in that position for several hours. Dinnertime had come and gone, but she hadn't been interested in food. She was hiding, she willingly admitted to herself. Hiding from Rhys, hiding from her past, hiding from her own raw confusion. She was so safe here, surrounded by her memories and her grandmother's things. She wondered hazily if she'd ever find the courage to step out of the snug haven again.

She hugged Flower to her until the cat struggled restlessly and jumped down, heading off in the direction of her food dish. Angie looked after her wistfully. There was only one problem with this cozy sanctuary, she thought. Loneliness. And not just for anyone. She was lonely for Rhys. It wasn't hard to imagine herself being held in his arms at that moment, and the vividness of the mental picture made her ache dully for it to be fact.

Was he lonely? she wondered suddenly, gnawing on her already teeth-marked lower lip. Was he sitting in that sparsely furnished, eerily quiet house of his thinking of her? Feeling badly about what he'd done, wondering if she'd ever be able to forgive him?

That she would forgive him was something she never doubted. Of course she'd been angry with him at first, angry and hurt. Knowing he'd paid a stranger to look into her past made her very uncomfortable. But, being Rhys, he would have seen his actions as the most direct method of finding out what he wanted to know. He hadn't been motivated by cruelty or mere curiosity, but by his concern for her. Knowing that, how could she remain angry with him?

She loved him, she thought with a pang of need. She loved him so very much. She *should* be angry with him, but instead she was touched that he'd been worried about her. His action had been typically arrogant, undeniably invasive, even clumsy, but no one else had gone to such trouble for her in longer than she could remember.

He'd had so little experience with caring about someone, with having someone care for him. He desperately needed the love she felt for him, even if he never truly learned how to return it. Again, she found herself being seduced by the feeling of being needed, really needed for the first time in her life.

Maybe—just maybe she could teach him about loving, teach him about sharing, she thought with the first spark of optimism. She didn't know a great deal about either one of them herself, considering her background, but she'd had her grandparents as an example of what a relationship could be with time and effort. Her past hadn't seemed to matter to him. If that wasn't standing between them, then all she had to battle was his natural caution and her own insecurity.

That was *all*? She almost smiled then, for the first time since she'd stumbled into her house after escaping the office.

Still, they had a chance. But only if she kept the lines of communication open between them. She couldn't accomplish anything, couldn't help either of them, by hiding herself away. Spurred by a new surge of determination, she stood, untying her robe as she headed for her bedroom.

RHYS MADE a futile effort to relax by having a warm shower and changing into a comfortable gray fleece running suit. He'd been trying to concentrate on *The Wall Street Journal* when his doorbell rang at just past nine that evening. He was startled but had no question who he'd find on his doorstep. His pulse increasing in anticipation, he threw open the door.

Angelique stood there looking very young and vulnerable in a soft pink sweater, worn, faded jeans and scuffed sneakers, her fine blond hair caught into a loose ponytail tied with a pink ribbon. "You were right, Rhys," she told him huskily, her hands twisting nervously at her waist. "I can't always handle everything alone. I need you."

He held out his arms and she stepped into them. "I'm here for you, Angelique," he murmured, his voice rough.

Snuggling into the soft fleece of his shirt, she sighed at the pleasure of hearing those words for the first time in so very long. Maybe it wouldn't be forever, she warned herself, but he was here for her now. She couldn't complain.

"Do you want to talk?" he asked, drawing her more fully into the house.

She hesitated only a moment. And then she smiled and slipped her hands beneath his top. "No."

His chest expanded beneath her palms as he inhaled sharply. "Oh."

Sliding her hands slowly down his chest until the tips of her fingers slipped beneath the band of his pants, she looked up at him in teasing challenge. "Would *you* rather talk?"

He cleared his throat forcefully. "Are you kidding?"

She moved her hands lower. She had just discovered the extent of his arousal when his control broke and he swung her into his arms. "If you only knew what you do to me," he muttered, heading toward the stairs with long, impatient strides.

Clinging trustingly, Angie rested her head on his shoulder and closed her eyes, knowing he'd soon show her exactly what she did to him. Content for now with knowing that the bond between them was more than physical, despite the desire that flared so hotly between them. She didn't waste time worrying about how long it would last or whether she would survive its end. At the moment, she had better things to think about. Better things to do....

FOR THE NEXT TWO WEEKS, Angie and Rhys were together quite a bit away from the office. As if to prove he wasn't embarrassed to be seen with her, Rhys took her to restaurants, the theater, a baseball game. Once or twice they ran into someone from the office. Angie knew tongues must be wagging furiously, but for once she didn't really care. If that was her price for spending time with Rhys, then she'd gladly pay it. Besides, she thought with grim humor, she was used to being the subject of gossip.

Angie was continually surprised by discoveries she made about Rhys. Though he hadn't allowed himself much time for movies in the past few years—or any other purely entertainment diversions—he enjoyed them a great deal, particularly sophisticated comedies and adventures. She rented several of the latest videos for him, then spent more time enjoying his obvious pleasure in the films than watching them herself.

She opened a cabinet in his den one day to uncover an extensive collection of vintage rock albums beneath an expensive stereo system. "I didn't know you liked music so much!" she exclaimed.

He looked up a bit sheepishly from the news magazine he'd been reading. "Yeah," he admitted. "I usually have some music going when I'm here by myself."

"Why didn't you tell me?"

He shrugged. "Guess it never came up."

She flipped through the collection, fascinated with the variety. The Beatles, The Rolling Stones, Elvis, Buddy Holly, The Doors, Joe Cocker, Country Joe and the Fish—and dozens more, most of whom she'd heard of, some she hadn't. "Seems like your collection stops about the time disco came into style," she commented teasingly.

He groaned. "No kidding. There hasn't been anything decent recorded since."

She spun on one heel, ready to do battle. "Bull," she said inelegantly. "There's been a lot of good music in the past ten years."

"Most of it by the same groups who've been recording since the sixties," he retorted, tossing the magazine aside and getting into the spirit of the good-natured argument. "The Stones, The Beach Boys, Tina Turner, The Who, Rod Stewart."

"Bon Jovi, AC/DC."

"You've got to be kidding."

"Now, come on, you've got some heavy metal stuff in here. Led Zeppelin, Iron Butterfly."

"Classics," he pronounced loftily.

She tilted her head defiantly and planted her hands on the hips of her color-washed jeans. "Madonna," she threw at him.

He groaned and shuddered dramatically. "Compared to Tina Turner? Why don't you list Barry Manilow while you're at it?"

"I *like* Barry Manilow," she informed him coolly, fighting a smile.

"You also like pineapple on pizza. We've already ascertained that your taste is rather questionable."

She gasped in mock outrage and threw herself at him, landing on his lap with enough force to make his breath escape in a whoosh. "Arrogant rat," she muttered, looping her arms around his neck. "Might I also remind you that I like *you*? What does *that* say about my tastes?"

"Some people might say that's a sure indication that you're weird," he answered lightly, his arms going around her waist to hold her on his knees.

"*They're* the ones with questionable tastes," she answered before tugging his mouth to hers and kissing him deeply.

He was smiling when she finally released him. "You have a great way of winning an argument, you know that?"

Smiling in return, she snuggled closer. "I really am

surprised that you're a closet rock-and-roll fan. I would have guessed you liked classical music."

"Image," he returned. "I try to look like the type who'd like classical because it's more respectable and impressive. But give me Eric Clapton any day." He paused, then added for emphasis, "I almost went to Woodstock."

She giggled, trying to picture him with shoulder-length hair and love beads. "Why didn't you?"

He shrugged against her cheek. "Uncle Sam wrote me that summer. He wouldn't give me time to stop by Woodstock on my way to 'Nam."

Her laughter vanished. "Were you frightened?" she asked quietly.

His voice became grim. "More times than I want to admit."

"How old were you?"

"Eighteen."

She swallowed. "So young."

"Yeah, well, I grew up fast." Another moment of silence and then he groaned. "Ah, hell."

She lifted her head inquiringly. "What?"

The look he gave her was rueful. "I just figured out how old *you* were that summer. You don't even remember Woodstock, do you? Or Vietnam or the first moonwalk or the Kennedy assassination."

"I wasn't born when Kennedy was killed, I was four when Woodstock and the moonwalk took place and I was nine when our troops came back from Vietnam," she answered. "I remember that—a little."

"Four," he repeated glumly. "I was guarding my ass in a ditch full of mud, watching my buddies get blown to bits, and you were still in diapers."

"I was not in diapers at four!" she denied heatedly.

"It was a figure of speech," he explained with a sigh. "You were in nursery school."

"Well, yes." She couldn't deny that one.

His expression was suddenly very distant. "Sometimes I forget how young you are."

"Does that bother you?" she asked in surprise.

"Only when I think about it."

"It doesn't matter, Rhys. We have a lot in common, despite the age difference. We both like music."

"Mmm."

"I'm sure we could find lots of songs we both like," she replied to his skeptical murmur. "You have several albums I like. We both enjoy adventure movies—and we're both terrible workaholics," she added with a slight smile.

Beginning to look a bit more cheerful, he conceded that one.

"And then there's this," Angie murmured, her hand slipping to the back of his head as she pulled his mouth to hers once more.

The kiss was long, deep, powerful.

"Yes," Rhys muttered roughly when it finally ended. "There is that." And then he kissed her again, bearing downward until they were both lying on the couch, his hand already working at the buttons of her striped cotton blouse.

THEY DID NOT TALK of their relationship during those two pleasant weeks, nor did they mention the future. Angie wasn't exactly sure whether that was her choice, his or mutual cowardice. She only knew they both seemed very careful to avoid any such serious discussions.

They began to plan their trip to visit Aunt Iris. Angie

was looking forward to it, though she expected a certain amount of awkwardness if the woman pressed for the exact nature of the relationship between her former foster son and his assistant. Still, she wanted to meet the woman who'd been so good to Rhys, who'd made such a difference in his life. Who'd given him the potential to learn how to love. Having talked to Aunt Iris several times during those two weeks, Rhys assured her that his foster mother was as excited about the upcoming meeting as Angie.

Only once during those almost idyllic days did any tension arise between Angie and Rhys. Dragging himself out of her bed early one morning so that he could go home to change clothes before reporting to the office, he grumbled, "This is getting old. It would be a hell of a lot easier if you'd just move in with me."

The words stunned her. Move in with him? she thought in what almost felt like sheer panic. Leave her grandmother's house? No! She couldn't. "I don't think we're quite ready for that step," she managed evenly enough.

Rhys didn't particularly like her answer—or the near-terror in her eyes at the mere suggestion. He sensed her reluctance to leave her cozy sanctuary and found himself resenting it. It wasn't as if he'd asked her to sell the old place, he thought. It was just that he wanted her with him, day and night, and his house was larger, nicer and in much better shape. It made sense to him that they could live there together. He didn't press, however. Something told him it wouldn't be wise, that their relationship was still too tentative, too fragile.

But there would come a time, he told himself in determination, when he'd make the suggestion again.

And he intended to make sure that time came soon. He was tired of waking up alone, even on the few mornings when he and Angie had not spent the night together. She was his. It was time she began to realize it.

JUNE ENTERED the meeting room so unobtrusively that only Angie noticed her at first. She frowned in question at the secretary's action, her hand stilling on her notepad as Rhys continued to speak to the associates gathered around the huge conference table. It must be awfully important for June to interrupt this crucial meeting, she thought with a sudden, indefinable sense of foreboding.

Her expression deeply troubled, June slipped Angie a note, then turned away and hurried out of the room. Her anxiety increasing, Angie steeled herself and opened the folded sheet of paper. What could have put that look onto June's usually smiling face?

Her eyes closed a moment later on a wave of grief. Grief for a woman she'd never met—and for Rhys, who would be devastated.

Rhys surprised everyone by suddenly stopping in midsentence and staring at Angie. "Angelique?" he demanded, forgetting for the first time to call her the more formal Ms. St. Clair in front of their associates. "What's wrong?"

She took a deep breath and stood, the note clutched in her hands, wondering how to get him in private to break the news. He settled that by taking the paper out of her nerveless fingers and opening it.

Angie was all the more distressed by the fact that Rhys's expression didn't change at all as he scanned the few words. The only sign of emotion she could detect was a sudden tightening around his mouth. Her heart ached for him, knowing how much suffering was locked behind that implacable mask of his.

Neatly folding the paper along its original lines, Rhys nodded to her and slipped it into his pocket. "Now, about the new conveyor system..." he began, ignoring the questioning silence in the room.

Too shocked to remember discretion, Angie exclaimed, "Rhys! You surely don't intend to go on with this meeting now."

He gave her a quick frown, more conscious than she of the stunned looks she was getting. "Yes, Ms. St. Clair, I do. There's no reason to postpone it."

As far as she was concerned, she and Rhys were the only ones in the room. "No reason?" she repeated, stepping so close to him that they stood toe to toe. "How can you say that?"

"There's nothing I can do now," he said gently. "Nothing anyone can do."

"You can grieve for her," Angie whispered, lifting a hand to his hard cheek. "Or if not for her, for yourself."

"Angelique—"

She turned her head abruptly, glancing around at the avidly curious faces surrounding them. "Mr. Wakefield has had a death in his family. I'm sure you'll understand that he needs time alone. We'll reconvene the meeting in a couple of days."

Shifting in their seats, the uncertain employees looked to Rhys for confirmation. He hesitated, then nodded curtly. "June will let you know the new time. That will be all for today."

No one wasted time leaving the room. Less than five minutes later, Angie and Rhys were alone. "You're the only person alive I'd let get away with a stunt like that," he told her flatly, hands on his hips as he loomed over her, visibly tense. "Talk about usurping my authority! Why did you—"

Ignoring the perfunctory lecture, she slid her arms around his waist and held him tightly. "I'm sorry, Rhys. So very sorry."

"Ah, hell." The unnatural stiffness left him along with his deep exhale. His arms went around her, his cheek resting against her hair. "I talked to her the day before yesterday. She sounded all right. If I'd known she was worse, I'd have gone to her."

"I know. But the note said she died in her sleep last night. Maybe no one knew the end was so close."

"I suppose not." He stood quietly for a long moment, holding her, before saying softly, "I was going to take you to her next week. You would have liked her, Angelique."

Tears streaming unheeded down her cheek, Angie nodded against his chest. "I'm sure I would have loved her," she murmured.

"Damn, I'm going to miss her."

Angie caught her breath on a sob. "I know. You must feel the same way I did when I lost my grandmother."

"As if you'd lost a part of yourself?" he asked huskily.

She turned her face upward, making no effort to hide the tears. "Yes. A very special part."

He lowered his head to rest his forehead against hers. "You're crying for me again."

"I can't help it," she admitted, knowing he wasn't a man who could cry for himself, wishing her tears could ease his pain. "I can't stand it that you're hurting. I wish I could help you."

"You are," he whispered huskily, brushing his lips very gently across hers. "Thank you."

Pressing her damp cheek to his throat, she stood on tiptoes to hug as much of him as she could reach, knowing that the most valuable thing she could do for him was simply to hold him. There hadn't been enough hugs in this man's life, no one to hold him when he'd hurt. Perhaps part of the reason had been that he hadn't encouraged such intimacy. Angie knew him well enough by now to understand that one couldn't wait for such encouragement from Rhys. She gave without asking—and he accepted with touching gratitude. For now, they both received what they needed from the relationship. She refused to think about what might lie ahead in their future.

AT IRIS'S REQUEST, there would be no funeral, so there was no reason for Rhys to leave town. They spent a quiet evening, sharing a dinner they'd prepared together, then sitting in his den and listening to music, arms entwined as they savored the time together. And when Rhys turned to her with pain in his eyes and a deep, aching need for her, Angie opened her arms to him, offering her body and her passion as comfort. He accepted both, making love to her with a special tenderness that brought tears to her eyes. And then they slept, wrapped together in his big bed. Angie woke only once during the night to find herself held tightly against Rhys's heart. Smiling in drowsy contentment at the position, she snuggled closer and went back to sleep.

10

RHYS WOULD HAVE BEEN the first to admit that he wasn't in the greatest mood. He couldn't say what was wrong, exactly—well, yes, he could, he thought with a scowl, his foot growing heavier on the accelerator. Angelique was driving him crazy with her stubborn refusal to move in with him. It was late, he was tired and he should be going home to spend a restful, pleasant evening with his woman. Instead, he was about to pass her house on the way to his own empty, lonely place several hours after ordering her to call it a day.

Some guys worried about other men as rivals for their lovers' affections. Rhys was grimly aware that his only competition was a house full of rose-colored, risk-free memories.

Even after all they'd shared in the month since Aunt Iris had died, even with the passion that grew stronger every time they were together, Angie still couldn't trust him—or herself—enough to abandon her sanctuary and risk building a future with him. What would it take, he wondered, turning the car onto her street, to make her feel as secure with him as she did with her precious mementos?

Dusk was settling over the neighborhood, casting long purple shadows across the neatly groomed lawns. Lights flickered to life—on street poles, yard and porch lamps, behind the curtains of the homes he passed. A denim-clad mother stepped onto a porch to call her children inside for the night. Skateboards under their arms, two boys bade good-night to their friends and sprinted in her direction. It was a traditional suburban, middle-class neighborhood—the kind of place Rhys had once fantasized of living in, complete with a mother in an apron and pearls, a father always available for a game of catch or a long talk, one-point-three siblings, a dog and a station wagon.

He could see why Angelique would feel secure here.

Was that what she needed? he asked himself suddenly, hands tightening on the steering wheel. Marriage? Children? The permanence implied by a legal license and a gold band?

His eyes on her house just ahead, he chewed thoughtfully on his lower lip. The idea of her as his partner in life as well as at the office was very tempting. He rather fancied the idea of introducing her as "my wife, Angelique." He couldn't help wondering if his background had left him with any chance of being successful at marriage and—he gulped—parenthood.

He'd never even considered marriage before, figuring he'd be predestined for failure. Only now could he see how much he'd been consumed by his work, how little time he'd given to anything else. He'd made that business his wife, his family. But, now with Angelique, maybe...

Impulsively he spun the wheel, guiding the car into her driveway. He hadn't intended to stop—hadn't even been invited to do so, actually—but here he was. All she could do was shut the door in his face, and she'd damned well better not.

"Rhys! I wasn't expecting you." Angie stood in the doorway, her freshly scrubbed face questioning, hair still damp from a shower, petite body wrapped into a soft robe. Her cat peeped out from behind the floor-length garment to greet him with a soft meow.

This is the way it should be, Rhys realized abruptly. When work was done, he and Angelique should be together, relaxed, comfortable, at home. If only he could convince her that her home was with him. "Are you going to let me in?"

She stood back, allowing him to enter, closing the door slowly behind him when he'd stepped past her. "You look tired," she said, evidently deciding to accept his presence without further comment. "Would you like a drink? How about something to eat?"

"Have you eaten?"

"I had a salad. But I'll make you something."

"A tuna sandwich sounds good," he hinted.

She smiled. "You're in luck. I happen to have a can of tuna."

"Thanks. I'll get my own drink." He headed for the refrigerator, where she'd gotten into the habit of keeping a supply of fruit-flavored soft drinks for him. He was in the mood for a grape soda. And Angelique. He thought he'd better concentrate on the soda first.

Popping the top on the can, he took a step back, then stumbled as he almost tripped over Flower. "Damn cat," he muttered without heat, reaching for a paper towel to wipe up the soda he'd splattered on the floor.

"Is she all right?" Angie asked in concern, whirling to check on her indignant pet.

"She's fine," Rhys answered wryly. "And so am I. Thanks so much for asking."

She chuckled. "I figured you could take care of yourself."

Soiled paper towel in hand, he opened the cabinet

where she kept her wastebasket. "I was attacked from behind. Blindsided. Taken completely unaware."

Smiling, she stood on tiptoe to kiss his cheek. "Poor baby. Want some chips with your sandwich?"

He stood as if frozen in the position of tossing the towel. "I—uh—what?"

Giving him an odd look, she repeated, "Would you like some chips, Rhys?"

"Oh. Yeah, thanks." *Damn*, but she was dangerous. All it had taken was a kiss on the cheek and a seductive murmur to reduce him to stammering incoherence. Any man who didn't take immediate steps to make a woman like that his forever was a fool. Rhys Wakefield had been called many things, but never a fool.

Remembering the towel, he leaned over to throw it away. He was just about to close the cabinet door when he noticed the envelope on the floor. It looked as though it had been dropped carelessly at the trash container, but had missed. Bending, he picked it up, noting the neat handwriting, the return address and the fact that it hadn't been opened.

"Did you mean to throw this away?" he asked, guessing that the letter was from her father.

She glanced at the envelope in his hand and frowned, then turned to set his plate on the table. "Yes, I did. Your dinner's ready."

"It's from your father, isn't it?"

"Yes. Throw it away, please."

"Angelique—"

"Rhys." Her eyes met his squarely, and there was no misinterpreting the hands-off look she gave him. "There's nothing my father has to say that I would be interested in hearing—or reading."

"Maybe he's just lonely," Rhys suggested carefully.

He wasn't sure why he was pushing her, but something told him that Angie would never be completely happy until she'd reconciled—at least partially—with her only surviving relative.

"Tough," she answered, her voice harder than he'd ever heard it. "He's lying in the bed he made for himself. If it's not as comfortable as he'd hoped, then it's his own fault for not being a bit more discriminating in his actions."

Rhys pulled out a chair and slung one leg over it, scooting up to the table and taking a bite of the sandwich. He chewed, swallowed, then risked one more comment. "I realize that he made some mistakes. But he's not the first, and he won't be the last. You said that your childhood wasn't particularly unhappy. Don't you have any feeling left for him?"

"He shattered any feelings I may have had," she muttered, sitting stiffly in the other chair. "The things he did—the things he said to me—I'll never let myself forget them."

Rhys set the half-eaten sandwich on the plate. "Are you always this unforgiving?"

Her eyes widened in wounded indignation. "Why are you pushing me about this?" she demanded. "What does it matter to you?"

He didn't like her wording. His clipped tone probably told her so. "I can't help wondering if you'll be this unmerciful if I do something that disappoints you."

"Rhys! How can you say that?" she scolded incredulously. "You'd never do anything like my father did. You're probably the most honest person I've ever met, both in business and your personal life. No one could ever compare you to my father."

"We all make mistakes, Angelique," he repeated

doggedly. "I can't promise that I'll never hurt you unintentionally or let you down in some way. If I do, will you be this eager to walk away, to sever our relationship?"

She looked at him for a long, taut moment, then reached out to touch his hand with the tips of her fingers. "I don't think I could ever walk away from you," she whispered.

He caught her hand in his, chest tightening. *Now*, a little voice inside him urged. *Do it now. Before you lose your nerve.*

"Then let's make it permanent," he urged gruffly, unable to be diplomatic when so much was at stake with her answer. "Marry me, Angelique."

She gasped, her hand going limp with shock. "Marry—?"

His fingers tightened convulsively around hers. She couldn't have looked more stunned if he'd reached across the table and slapped her, he thought grimly. "We belong together. Not just for an affair or an office romance. For always. I need you in my life. I care a great deal for you. Say you'll marry me."

Her throat worked with her swallow. Her voice was hoarse. "Rhys, I wasn't expecting this. You'll have to give me more time."

"How long?" he asked evenly, his eyes never leaving hers.

She shifted restlessly in her chair, though he refused to release her hand. "I don't know! I can't give you a time and a date."

"I want an answer, Angelique. And I'm not long on patience."

She gave a wry grimace. "Believe me, I'm aware of that."

He brought her hand to his cheek, his voice husky in reaction to that fleeting moment of intimate humor. "Marry me."

Her eyes squeezed closed for a moment, then opened to expose tears in their violet depths. "Rhys, please. It means a lot to me that you've—"

He glared at her, irritation surging through him. "Don't you *dare* give me the song and dance about being flattered that I asked and this is such an honor," he warned.

She sighed, annoyance showing briefly in her face. "Let me finish. And, dammit, it *is* an honor, whether you want to hear it or not. You think I don't know what a marriage proposal means to you? How could you expect me to treat it so lightly that I could answer without even giving it any thought?"

"I guess I was kind of hoping you'd already given it some thought," he admitted somewhat sheepishly. Had he been an idiot to assume that marriage had crossed her mind simply because it had his own? Had she never even considered making their relationship permanent? If not, he thought, mouth tightening stubbornly, then it was time she did.

Her cheeks darkened. "I suppose the thought has...occurred to me a time or two," she confessed softly.

His voice gentled as he relaxed in momentary relief. So she *was* as involved as he. "And was it distasteful to you?" he asked, trying not to sound as vulnerable as he felt with the question.

"No. Not distasteful. But...frightening."

He frowned. "I frighten you?"

"The thought of taking a step that drastic frightens me," she corrected him. With a sharp tug, she pulled her hand from his and laced it with her other, tightly enough that the knuckles went white. "Try to understand, Rhys."

"I will—if you'll tell me what frightens you."

She seemed to make an effort to organize her thoughts. "Last year my entire world turned upside down. I lost everything I had, my grandmother, my respect for my father, nearly all my possessions. It left me lost and scared and wondering who I was and what I was worth as a person. So I came here, and I built a new life for myself. I took a job for which I had no training and I managed to do well in it."

"Damned well."

She smiled weakly at his interjection, then continued. "Then you and I started seeing each other and I...I fell in love with you. But," she added hastily, when he leaned forward eagerly and started to speak, "I'm not at all sure that I'm ready to change the way things are now. I'm happy now, content. I'm afraid to risk losing everything again by acting unwisely, without taking the time to make sure what we—*both* of us, Rhys—understand exactly what we're doing."

"I know what I'm doing. You're the one who's scared." He swept his hand in a half circle around him. "You've made yourself a safe little hideaway here. Oh, you come out occasionally, until things get a little too uncomfortable, until it looks as though you'll have to start taking a few risks again. And then you rush back here to hide with your cat and your things. I haven't asked you to give up anything, Angelique. You can keep this house, you can keep everything in it. Your job won't be affected, I won't ask you to stop seeing the friends you've made in the past few months. I'll even accept the cat as part of the package."

He leaned forward, urgency making him tense and somewhat rough. "You say you love me, but you're afraid to trust me, to trust what we've found together. Until you do, we don't have a prayer of making this thing work."

"I need some time, Rhys," she almost pleaded. "Please don't give me ultimatums."

He snorted. "Ultimatums?" he repeated, unable to keep a hint of bitterness from his voice. "You mean like marry me or it's over?"

She nodded apprehensively.

Rhys shook his head. "No. Even if I thought it would work, I wouldn't use that one. It would be a bluff, anyway. There's no way in hell I'm going to let you go now that I've found you. Even if I have to keep storming this fortress of yours until you finally admit that you don't stand a chance against me."

Her smile was tentative, tremulous. "I think I'm already aware of that."

He forced himself to relax, picking up the remainder of his sandwich. "You've got your time, Angelique. But don't wait too long."

Or I'll have to do something rash, he added to himself. *Kidnapping sounds like a good start. Or maybe I'll just get you pregnant. You'd look good carrying my baby, lady.* Prudently remaining silent out of certain knowledge that she'd go for his throat if he voiced those particular chauvinistic thoughts, Rhys smiled ferally and finished his dinner.

ANGIE GASPED and arched upward when Rhys sank his teeth delicately into the soft inner flesh of her thigh. If his intention was to drive her insane tonight, he was doing an excellent job, she thought dazedly. She'd long since lost track of the time that had passed after he'd slipped the robe from her body and laid her gently on the bed. There was no part of her that he hadn't stroked, kissed, teased, pleasured. She was no longer even capable of participating in the lovemaking, having been reduced to quivering, writhing, gasping semiconsciousness.

The tip of his tongue shot out to soothe the faint marks left by his teeth. His hands cupped her bottom, holding her in place as his mouth stroked across her thigh and then moved inward to nibble at the vulnerable spot just above the golden curls between her legs. Nuzzling into those curls, he used his tongue once more to taste and torment her, flicking rapidly at the swollen, aching flesh until she cried out and bowed sharply upward, certain that she was going to lose her mind if he didn't stop. Equally certain that she'd die if he did.

"Rhys. Oh, *Rhys*." If she'd had any breath left, the words would have been very close to a scream. As it was, they were a mere whisper.

He heard them. Surging up her body, he pressed his mouth to hers. "Tell me again," he muttered without raising his head.

She knew what he wanted to hear. It wasn't the first time he'd demanded to hear them since he'd brought her to bed. "I love you," she murmured into his mouth. "I love—"

His tongue surged inside, tasting the words, swallowing them. His hand closed over her breast as his body merged with hers, his hips already flexing to begin the rhythm that would carry her back into the maelstrom of passion. Her fingernails sinking into his shoulders, Angie moaned in pleasure and abandoned herself to his lead.

Her knees clenched high on his hips, she arched to take him deeper. She moaned, gasped, cried his name. Sobbed in relief and disappointment when the crest broke and she shivered in fulfillment, knowing that the end had been inevitable, wanting only to prolong it. She was never more happy than when locked with Rhys in this intimate sharing, this total oblivion to anything but each other.

"Angelique, I—" His words died in a groan as his long, taut body shuddered in a climax that seemed to rock the bed beneath her.

She wished he'd finished the sentence. Had he wanted to tell her he loved her? If so, it would have been the first time, though he had seemed insatiable to hear the words from her. She knew how hard it would be for him to say those words—even harder than proposing had been, she thought, stroking his damp, heaving back as he lay half across her, recovering his strength. It would be especially hard for him to say them if he was still unsure of her.

He'd asked her to marry him. Closing her eyes, Angie took a deep breath.

"Am I crushing you?" Rhys asked immediately, shifting his weight.

"No," she assured him, holding him more tightly. "I'm fine."

He murmured something she didn't quite catch and settled his head more comfortably on her breast, seemingly content to lie still and have her stroke him.

Turning back to her thoughts, Angie tried to imagine what it would be like to be married to Rhys. He'd accused her of not trusting him. He was wrong, of course. During the past months, she had learned that there was no one on earth she trusted more than Rhys. He wouldn't let her down in the way her father had, lie to her as her former friends and lovers had done. He wouldn't be unfaithful to her. To Rhys, a marriage vow would be his word. To break his word would be to lose the honor that was so very important to him, having been all he had for so long.

So what *was* she afraid of?

Losing him, she answered herself almost immediately. Not to another woman, not to a prison cell, but to disinterest. To habits formed years earlier, shaped by years of seeking and striving for acceptance. Having him finally admit that the novelty of being loved had worn off, that his business provided all the daily stimulation he required.

Perhaps she was still struggling with her own sense of failure, with her own doubts about what she had to offer to a man such as Rhys. He was older, more experienced, more successful, more confident in his abilities. Would he grow tired of someone who'd been in nursery school while he'd fought in Vietnam, who'd led a sheltered, shallow, self-gratifying life until forced by circumstances to reevaluate her priorities and change her ways? Whose very name carried a stigma of dishonor?

Rhys breathed deeply and rolled onto his back, pulling her with him until she lay against his shoulder, his arm snugly around her. "Tell me again," he ordered, a faint smile creasing his weary face.

"I love you, Rhys," she complied willingly. He seemed to need to hear the words as often as she would say them.

He needed her. Knowing he couldn't see her, she

made a face at her own vulnerability. She knew she wouldn't be as susceptible to anyone else's need, but being needed by strong, self-sufficient, dauntingly proud Rhys was something she simply couldn't resist. Nor would she ever be able to resist him. He'd been absolutely correct earlier. Despite her fears, Angie had long since conceded the futility of defying him. If he'd set his mind on marrying her, they would be married. She hadn't the strength—nor the desire—to refuse him something so important to him.

"I'll marry you, Rhys."

The quietly spoken words galvanized him from satiated dozing to full awareness. "You will?"

"Yes."

He shifted until he was resting on one elbow, leaning over her, his gray eyes fixed intently on her face. "You just this minute decided?"

She smiled faintly. "Yes."

"Why?"

The corners of her smile deepened. Trust Rhys to look so suspicious of her sudden capitulation, she thought. "Because I love you, Rhys. And because I want to. Okay?"

He grinned and kissed her. "Okay," he repeated when he lifted his head. "When?"

"There's no real hurry, is there?" she hedged, unwilling to get into that specific planning just yet.

His grin changed rapidly into a frown. "Angelique," he said warningly.

She sighed. "Rhys, I'm not backing out and I'm not leading you on. I simply don't want to rush something so important. I want to take our time and do it right. There are a few things I need to do first, all right?"

He nodded, though still not looking completely satisfied. "I guess I can understand that. What are you going to do about this house?"

"I don't know yet," she admitted.

"There's no rush," he said in unconscious imitation of her. "We'll come up with a workable solution. In the meantime, there are a few repairs I'd like to make. I worry about you living here with some of the things that are wrong with this house. I'd like the wiring checked and the plumbing and—"

She put her hand over his mouth. "You think I'm going to suddenly agree to let you pay for all this now that we're unofficially engaged?" she demanded.

He pulled her hand firmly away. "The engagement is very much official," he informed her flatly. "And, yes, I expect you to let me foot some of the bills. I've got the money and, as my wife, half that money will be yours. Hell, you could have all of it if you wanted it. And don't get defensive," he added with indulgent resignation, "I know you're not marrying me for my money."

"No, I'm not."

"You let me help you with a few repairs around here and I'll let you take your time about setting a wedding date," he promised wickedly. "Within reason, of course."

"You are a shameless hustler," she informed him sternly, loving the laughter in his usually hard eyes. Hard for everyone else. So very warm and gentle for her.

"Not thinking of changing your mind already, are you?" he murmured, lowering his head to nibble at the upper curve of her left breast.

"No. But I may start trying to reform you," she replied, fingers already slipping into his thick silver hair.

"Be my guest," he invited, then took the tip of her breast into his mouth.

Angie inhaled sharply and closed her eyes. "Later," she murmured distracted. "I'll start...later."

11

Rhys wanted to buy her an engagement ring during lunch the next day. Angie convinced him to wait until the weekend, when they'd have more time to shop. It wasn't as easy to convince him to allow her a couple of nights alone during the remainder of the week. He saw no reason for them to continue to maintain separate residences now that she'd agreed to marry him. She knew both that and his impatience to get a ring on her finger were signs that he was still insecure in their relationship, still concerned that something would go wrong. With his past, she understood his reservations.

Emotional baggage, she'd heard it called. Fears and insecurities left over from past failures, past mistakes. Rhys had them. So did she. Having lost everything once before, she'd had a sample of the pain that would result from losing everything again—especially if everything included losing Rhys. She wanted so desperately to marry him, to make a future with him. And yet, what if she were being granted a glimpse of heaven only to have it snatched away from her? Was she strong enough, had she developed enough character during the past year to rebuild her life again if that happened?

Or would it destroy her this time?

"Listen, Angie, I hope you don't mind my asking," Gay began hesitantly during afternoon break on Friday. Most of the others had already returned to work, leaving only Gay, Darla, Angie and the shy Priscilla sitting around the formerly crowded table. "There's this rumor going around and, well, we can't stand not knowing if it's true. I've been elected to go to the source."

"What rumor?" Angie asked calmly, though she suspected she already knew, especially since she was so familiar with the formidable WakeTech grapevine.

Gay glanced at Darla, then almost shyly back at Angie. "Are you and Mr. Wakefield..." She hesitated as if concerned that the question were too absurd to even put into words. "Well, we heard the two of you had gotten engaged," she finished in a bold rush.

Cheeks warming a bit, Angie smiled weakly. "Where did you hear that?"

"From June," Gay admitted. "She says Mr. Wakefield told *her*. I've never known June to lie, but we thought maybe she was teasing us."

Angie took a deep breath. "She wasn't teasing. It's true."

"It's *true*?" Darla asked with a gasp. "You're going to marry Mr. Wakefield?"

Her smile deepening ruefully at the identical expressions of stunned disbelief surrounding her, Angie nodded. "Yes."

"Why?" Priscilla, the timid clerk-typist who'd more than once expressed nervous awe of her stern employer, clapped her hands over her mouth as soon as the word escaped her. "I'm sorry," she mumbled, flushing scarlet. "I—uh—just—er—"

"It's okay," Angie reassured the younger girl, rather amused. "I know Rhys seems a bit intimidating at times...."

"Oh, just a bit," Gay murmured, rolling her eyes comically at the understatement.

Angie joined in the ripple of laughter. "All right, a lot intimidating," she clarified. "But he's not, really. He's just..." She hesitated, trying to decide how to describe Rhys to people who'd never seen the softer, more vulnerable side of him. People who didn't know about a little boy who'd been left alone at night, who'd been abandoned and then neglected, who'd been sent to fight a war when he should have been dancing in the mud at Woodstock, who needed love so desperately that Angie couldn't resist him, no matter how cautious she'd tried to be.

"He's a little shy," she said at last, realizing for the first time that he was, indeed, rather shy. Afraid of being rejected. Defensive about his lack of family and formal education. Wary of lowering the barriers that had protected him in the past.

"Shy?" Gay repeated incredulously. "Mr. Wakefield?"

Darla shook her head. "Now that's an adjective I never would have applied to the boss."

Her hands lifting in a gesture of frustration, Angie made a wry face. "I know it's hard to believe, but you'd have to know him better to understand."

"And we can't get to know him better, because he doesn't let anyone get that friendly with him," Gay commented.

"I'm working on him," Angie promised.

"He *did* smile at me and say good morning yesterday when I passed him in the hall," Priscilla murmured cautiously. "It scared me so much I nearly dropped a whole armful of correspondence. I'd never seen him smile before."

Chuckling, Angie pushed her chair away from the table. "He has a gorgeous smile," she couldn't resist saying. "I'm trying to get him to use it more often."

Eyes widening, Gay caught Angie's wrist. "You're in love with the guy, aren't you?" she asked with characteristic tactlessness.

"Yes, I am," Angie replied gently.

"And he—?"

He still hadn't told her he loved her, Angie thought, biting her lip. "I'm working on that, too."

He loved her, she was sure. He *had* to love her. Perhaps someday he'd feel secure and comfortable enough to tell her. She hoped it would be soon. She'd discovered that she needed to hear the words as badly as he seemed to need to hear them from her.

Gay, Darla and Priscilla exchanged quick, concerned glances, then turned carefully reassuring smiles to Angie. "Of course he loves you," Darla said bracingly. "He'd be a fool not to."

Touched, Angie smiled. "Thanks. But I'd better get back to work now. Being engaged to him won't keep him from expressing extreme displeasure if he decides I'm goofing off on the job."

Still smiling, she turned and hurried away. She hadn't quite gotten out of range when Priscilla spoke to the other two, obviously unaware that Angie could still hear. "I sure hope she knows what she's doing. I'd hate to see her get hurt."

I know the feeling, Priscilla, Angie thought fervently. *Oh, yes, I do know the feeling.*

IMMERSED IN DETAILS for the production changes that would go into effect on Monday, Rhys worked late that evening. Angie stayed with him until he noticed that she was almost trembling with exhaustion. Then he ordered her to go home. She protested, saying he had to be as tired as she, but he stood firm, promising he'd only be a few minutes behind her.

"I'll go on to my place tonight," he said reluctantly. "That way I won't wake you when I come in. Get some sleep tonight. Next week's going to be a killer. And tomorrow," he added with a faint smile, "we're going ring shopping. I'm getting impatient to publicly stake my claim."

She made a face at the chauvinistic remark. He knew she'd have been more energetic about it if she hadn't been so tired. "You've already got everyone in the company talking about it," she told him with an attempt at sternness. "You should have known when you told June that you might as well have made a general announcement."

He grinned without a trace of shame. "I knew," he said simply. June could be implicitly trusted with business details, but she had a well-known weakness for gossip. Rhys had been fully aware of that weakness when he'd told her that he and Angie were to be married. There'd be no more engineers trying to manipulate their way into her bed, he thought in smug satisfaction. "Go home, Angelique. I'll pick you up in the morning, around ten."

Sighing, she picked up her purse and stood on tiptoe to kiss him. "Good night, Rhys. Don't stay too long, okay? You need to rest. And drive carefully. I worry about you when you're on the street so late and so tired."

He loved it when she fussed over him. He could quickly become spoiled to the novel treatment. "I'll be careful," he promised.

It was more than an hour later before Rhys made himself put everything away and follow Angie out of the now-deserted building. He thought longingly of her as he drove from the parking lot, headed for home. How he'd love to be in bed with her now, holding her against him as they slept. She was going to have to set the wedding date soon, he told himself on a surge of determination. Whatever lingering fears were causing her to hesitate would have to be resolved soon. He had no intention of spending many more nights alone.

Following the habit he'd developed during the past months, he drove the mile or so out of his way to pass her house on his way home. It must be exhaustion making him particularly uneasy tonight, he thought wearily. Pleased that she was getting some sleep, he noted that all her lights were out except for the one living room lamp she always left on when she was home alone. Not because she was afraid of the dark, she'd assured him earnestly when he'd teased her about it, but because she didn't want to bump into the furniture if she needed a drink of water in the middle of the night. He'd generously accepted her explanation without pointing out that she didn't bother to leave it on when he spent the night there.

Strongly tempted to pull into her driveway and risk an attempt to join her in the bed without disturbing her, he slowed as he approached. No, he thought reluctantly, he'd let her sleep. He'd be seeing her in a few hours, after all. They were going to buy the ring that would mark her as his. All his. For life. Whether he deserved her or not.

He'd never understand the premonition that kept him from driving on. His eyes narrowed intently on the aging frame structure, his throat tightening in a sudden grip of misgiving, he told himself he was being foolish. Obviously there was nothing wrong. He just didn't want to drive past.

The explosion rocked his car.

Cursing frantically, he yanked the wheel, pulling over to the side of the road. Even as he threw himself out the door, her house burst into flames.

"Angelique!" It was as close as he'd ever come to a scream.

The door was locked, of course. The key she'd given him was still dangling from the ignition with his other keys. The adrenaline rush of sheer panic gave him strength to kick in the door. "Angelique!"

The house was already a mass of rubble, an inferno of heat and smoke. He plowed furiously into it, calling her name again and again, heading in the general direction of the bedroom. Coughing, sweating, praying incoherently, he tore into a pile of splintered boards that had been her living room wall. The piano he'd once strained to move six inches leaned crookedly in his way. He shoved it aside without even being conscious of doing so.

"Don't let her be dead," he whispered hoarsely, coughing between words as the acrid smoke surrounded him. "Oh, *God*, don't let her be dead." If she was, he wanted nothing more than to die with her.

He found her half-buried, her legs pinned. His heart stopped when he saw her, lying so still, her golden hair matted with blood. Unaware of the tears rolling down his face until he was forced to dash a hand across his eyes to clear them, he knelt beside her, unconcerned for his own safety. "Angelique. I'm here, baby. Wake up, sweetheart. Show me you're all right. I love you, Angelique. Don't let me lose you now."

She stirred, moaning in shock and pain. He sobbed in relief that she was alive. "It's okay, sweetheart. I'm going to get you out of here," he told her, tearing into the rubble in frantic haste, knowing the shell of the house could collapse on them at any moment, choking on the smoke that would kill them if a falling beam didn't.

The air grew hotter as the fire crept closer, snapping hungrily at everything in its path. Rhys was soaked with sweat and tears, but his only concern was getting Angie out of the house and into the closest hospital.

Lifting her carefully, he struggled to his feet, still murmuring reassurances mixed with broken prayers. He was vaguely aware of the terrified cat that dashed past his feet toward the front door, meowing loudly, but he didn't stop. Something fell only inches behind him as he reached the yawning door. Sparks rained on the back of his neck, but he hardly noticed the tiny pinpoints of pain. His full concentration was on the nearly unconscious woman in his arms.

Hastily dressed neighbors gathered around him, steadying him as he stumbled off the porch, coughing, dragging air into burning lungs. Arms reached for Angelique, but he resisted them, lowering her to the ground a safe distance from the house. She moaned and his stomach tightened at the pain in the sound. He couldn't bear it that she was hurting.

He took anxious inventory of her injuries. Her legs were bloody and torn, possibly broken, there was a jagged cut on her forehead and a great deal of bruising. Her breathing was harsh from the smoke she'd inhaled, but steady enough to reassure him. He'd gotten to her ahead of the fire, so she hadn't been burned. She was obviously in shock, but something told him she'd suffered no internal injuries. She would live, he thought, sagging in nerveless relief.

Sirens grew closer, making themselves heard over the babble of voices and roar of flames. He welcomed the sounds, knowing they signaled help for Angelique. "Rhys?" she whispered, her head shifting restlessly on the ground.

"I'm here, baby," he said quickly, clasping her hand tightly in his as someone covered her with a blanket. "I'm here."

"Where's Flower?" a sleepy young voice demanded from close by. "Did anyone see Flower?"

Rhys glanced up at the boy who, dressed in Batman pajamas, hovered barefoot behind the woman who'd brought the blanket. He'd seen him before. Angie's little friend, Mickey, who'd given her the kitten.

He looked from Angelique to the burning house. She loved that damned cat. Slowly releasing her hand, he stood, his place beside her immediately taken by Mickey's mother. An ambulance squealed around the corner, followed by two fire trucks. Cursing himself for a fool, Rhys took a deep breath and ran toward the house.

"Hey!" someone shouted. "What's he doing? Stop him!"

Restraining hands gripped him, but Rhys shrugged them off. The cat had been just inside the door. He hoped it was too frightened to have moved. Ducking his head, his arm protecting his face, he dove inside.

"That man's gone back into the house, Mommy! Do you think he's gone to get Flower?"

"Oh, my God, he'll be killed!"

"Rhys?" Angie forced her burning eyes open, Kim's frightened gasp rousing her from the haze of pain and disorientation. "He went back in?" She struggled to sit up, the movement causing her to cry out in pain. Something was terribly wrong with her legs.

Kim's hands caught her shoulders, pressing her gently back to the ground. "No, Angie, lie still. I'm...I'm sure he'll be all right. Here's the ambulance. You'll be okay now."

"Rhys!" The name came out as a ragged croak, and then she was seized by a spell of deep coughs. Each one sent pain ricocheting through her body.

"Shh, take it easy, lady. Here, let me put this over your mouth. It'll help you breathe easier." A white-uniformed paramedic knelt beside her, slipping a clear mask over her face.

She could feel unconsciousness tugging at her, pulling her away from the pain and confusion. She fought it, fought the mask, clinging to the pain in an effort to stay alert. She had to know if Rhys was safe. She tried to call his name again, but the mask muffled her cry. And then a sharp pain in her arm made her sob in protest. Her grasp on consciousness loosened. Another wave of agony from her legs pushed her over the edge, Rhys's name trembling on her lips.

SHE'D ALWAYS REMEMBER the following hours only in snatches of half-conscious agony—spasms of pain, strange voices and bright lights, gentle hands that touched her and made her cry out in protest. Each time she tried to ask about Rhys, something was done to send her back into oblivion. At times she thought she heard his voice telling her over and over how much he loved her, but he was never there when she managed to open her eyes. All she saw were blurred, unfamiliar faces set in identical expressions of grave sympathy.

She needed him. She'd needed him when the house had crashed down around her, and he'd been there. Where was he now?

"That man's gone back into the house, Mommy!"

"Oh, my God, he'll be killed!"

"No," Angie sobbed, her head rolling helplessly against the thin, starchy pillow beneath it. "Rhys. Rhys!"

"She's still in pain," a gruffly concerned voice murmured above her. The same voice then proceeded to bark instructions. Knowing the medication he ordered would put her back to sleep, Angie tried to object but wasn't given the opportunity. She was still moaning Rhys's name when she went under again.

The next thing she heard was a low groan. It took her a few moments to realize the sound had come from her own raw throat. Forcing her eyes open, she frowned as she tried to orient herself. She was lying in a hospital bed, an IV needle taped to her arm. She wore a hospital gown, her lower half covered with a sheet, and both legs seemed to be elevated and immobilized. Her head hurt. Lifting her free hand cautiously to it, she felt the bandage on her forehead and sensed that a row of stitches lay beneath it. A plain round clock hung on the wall opposite the bed; she blinked to focus on it. Four-thirty. The sunlight streaming through the window on her left told her it was late afternoon. Saturday? she wondered, struggling to concentrate.

An explosion. A crash of wood and glass as her bedroom collapsed around and upon her. Pain. Heat. Rhys's voice begging her to be all right. More pain as he freed her from the debris and lifted her. A dash through heavy, smothering smoke. Fire.

She closed her eyes and tightened her throat against

a sob. Her house. Her grandparents' things. The porcelain figurines, the doilies and quilts and afghans, the ceramic dog in the foyer. Her drawings and photographs, the yellowed print of the *Last Supper*, furniture and memories. All gone. She'd lost everything again. Her grief was too deep for tears as she reflected on the unfairness of losing everything twice in one year. She wondered if she'd ever be able to piece her life back together a second time.

But, no. It wasn't quite the same this time. Her mind clearing, she pulled her lower lip between her teeth and opened her eyes.

This time she had Rhys to help her. This time there was someone to turn to, someone whose arms would be open to comfort her. Someone who—

Rhys! Gasping frantically, she turned her eyes wildly around the empty room, seeking him as she was assaulted by another memory of the chaotic aftermath of the explosion.

"That man's gone back into the house, Mommy! Do you think he's gone to get Flower?"

"Oh, my God, he'll be killed!"

"Rhys?" she whispered apprehensively, her fingers tightening on the thin crisp sheet. Rhys had pulled her out of the house. Had he—surely he hadn't gone back in for her pet. But it was exactly what he would have done, she realized, her chest tightening with fear. He would have done that for her. *Please,* she thought desperately. *Oh, please be all right.*

The house, the furnishings, the mementos no longer mattered to her. She could survive their loss. They were only things. But Rhys—*oh, Rhys, please.*

A quiet knock on the door brought her head around so quickly that she couldn't hold back the soft cry of pain, Rhys's secretary bustled in, her pleasant face creased with a worried frown. "Angie, honey, are you okay? Are you in pain? Should I call someone?"

Riding out the pounding in her temples, Angie held up an unsteady hand to stop the flow of questions. "It's okay, June. I just moved my head too quickly. Where is Rhys?" she demanded without pause, her heart seeming to stop to await the answer to that all-important question.

"He's resting in a room down the hall," June assured her. "The doctors had to threaten to sedate him to get him to leave your side for a while, but he was about to collapse on his feet."

Angie's heart resumed its beating with such force that she had to take several deep breaths to steady it. "He's all right?" she whispered, her eyes locked on June's face.

June smiled and patted her hand. "He's fine, dear. He has a few burns and bruises, but nothing serious."

"He was burned? Where? How badly?"

"He's fine, Angie," June repeated firmly. "You'll see for yourself very soon. I'm sure he'll be back in here the minute he wakes up." She shook her head in apparent wonder. "I've never seen Mr. Wakefield as distraught as he was when I first saw him this morning. I heard about the explosion on the radio and when I heard your name I rushed straight to the hospital. He was pacing up and down the waiting room while they operated on you. Wouldn't even let them treat his burns until he was sure you were going to be okay. He—"

"They operated on me?" Angie interrupted with a frown.

"No one's talked to you about your injuries yet?"

"I just woke up."

"Oh. Well, they had to put a pin in your left ankle. It was pretty badly broken. Your other leg's fractured, too, but I understand the damage wasn't too extensive. You're a very lucky young woman, Angie. It's a wonder you weren't killed. If Rhys hadn't happened to drive up when the explosion occurred, you probably would have been. I've heard of a few miracles in my lifetime, and that was one of them."

Her legs ached and her head throbbed dully. Angie fought the weakness, wanting to hear everything. "Did Rhys really go back into the house for my cat?"

June looked heavenward. "Yes, dear, he did. That's when he was burned, actually. But he saved her. Your neighbor was here and said her little boy's taking care of the cat for you until you're well."

Rhys was safe. And he'd saved Flower. Angie closed her eyes and offered a quick prayer of gratitude and an apology for complaining about the loss of a few possessions.

"I'm so pleased about your engagement, Angie," June told her warmly. "You've done wonders for Mr. Wakefield. He obviously loves you very deeply."

"I love you, Angelique. Don't let me lose you now."

Had he really said the words, or had they only been part of her half-delirious fantasies?

The door swooshed open again, and Angie looked around more cautiously this time, hoping to see Rhys. Instead, she found a doctor who hardly looked old enough to shave, his smooth, freckled face wreathed in a bright smile. "So you're awake, are you? It's about time. I'm Dr. Kent. How are you feeling?"

"I'll let you talk to your doctor now, but I'll be back later," June promised before slipping out.

"How is Rhys?" Angie demanded before the door had even closed behind her co-worker.

The doctor chuckled and shook his sandy head. "Honestly, the two of you! He wouldn't even let us treat him last night until you'd been taken care of, and now here you are asking about him before you even find out about your own injuries. It must be love."

She smiled. "It must be. So, how is he?"

"He's fine. I slipped him a pain medication to help him sleep. He'll probably be out for a couple more hours—long enough for me to make a safe escape, anyway," he added with a grin. "That's one intimidating man, you know that? It wasn't easy for the staff to treat you with him hanging over our shoulders threatening dire consequences if you weren't given the very best of care."

"That's Rhys," Angie admitted fondly, beginning to relax now that she had official confirmation that Rhys was all right. She listened quietly as the young doctor outlined her own injuries, telling her that her recovery would not be immediate and it would not be painless, but promising that she would eventually be as mobile as ever.

The informal conference was interrupted only once by a delivery of flowers from some of Angie's co-workers. The messages were warm, sympathetic and touching. She blamed her resulting tears on her weakness. Noting those tears and the trembling she couldn't quite control, Dr. Kent stood to leave. "Get some rest, Ms. St. Clair."

"Angie."

"I can increase your pain medication a bit if you need it, Angie."

She wasn't exactly comfortable, but she didn't want

to feel drugged again. "No, I don't need it. Thank you."

"All right. Call the nurse if the pain gets worse. I'll leave an authorization for medication."

"Thank you," she repeated, hoping it wouldn't be necessary. Her legs hurt—in fact, she decided grimly, her entire body hurt.

She wanted Rhys.

She got, instead, Gay and Darla, who entered cautiously, poking their heads into her door to see if she was awake. "Oh, Angie," Gay exclaimed, rushing in, her arms full of packages. "We're so sorry. How are you?"

"I've been better," Angie admitted wryly. "But I'm lucky to be alive. I'm not complaining."

"We won't stay long," Darla promised. "We had to see for ourselves that you were all right. The news report sounded so awful."

Angie tilted her head curiously, then wished she hadn't. Raising her hand to her temple in a vain attempt to massage the pain away, she asked, "What news report?"

"Both radio and television have covered the explosion and fire, describing the way Mr. Wakefield rescued you," Gay explained, her eyes round with awe. "You were so lucky that he arrived at exactly the right time." She didn't go on to ask why Rhys was arriving at Angie's house at that time of night, Angie noticed with weary amusement. "Anyway, we brought you some stuff. We know all your own things were destroyed, so we called some of the gang from the office and everyone chipped in to buy you some gowns and a robe and slippers, some undies and makeup, a few other things you'll be needing. If you need us to pick you up a couple of outfits to get you by until you can go shopping, just let us know, okay?"

For the second time in a hour, Angie's eyes filled with tears. "Thank you. That was so thoughtful of you."

Darla shrugged modestly. "We wanted to do it," she said simply. "It was all we knew to do to help."

Gay took a deep breath. "Angie, we wanted to tell you that we're really sorry about everything you've been through lately. We heard about your father. It was on the news during the report about the explosion at your house."

12

CHOKING ON A COUGH, Angie cleared her throat and asked weakly, "My—uh—my father? He was mentioned on the news?"

Gay flushed as Darla threw her an exasperated look. "Well—um—I guess one of the television reporters recognized your name or something. Or maybe they checked into your background when they heard you were engaged to Mr. Wakefield—he's pretty well-known in this area, you know. Anyway, they said your father had gotten into some trouble in Boston and he's—well, incarcerated. Now we understand why you've been so reluctant to talk about your past. But we want you to know it doesn't matter to us. I mean, gosh, everyone has a black sheep in the family. My uncle—"

"Gay," Darla interrupted with a pained expression. "Maybe you'd better just hush. Angie's tired. She needs to rest."

"You're right. We'll see you later, Angie. Be sure and call if you need anything, okay?"

Angie managed a smile. "Thanks, Gay. Darla."

Rhys burst into the room before they could leave. His hair was singed, sooty and wildly disarrayed, his once-white shirt smudged and torn, his expensive slacks beyond salvaging. He smelled of smoke and sported several neat white bandages. Angie thought he looked wonderful.

With barely a nod for her visitors, he crossed the room in three long strides and sank to the edge of the bed beside her. Her eyes locked with his stormy ones as he slipped a hand behind her head and lowered his mouth to hers. The kiss couldn't have been more gentle if she were made of spun glass. The breath he took when it ended was long, ragged, harsh. "Oh, God, Angelique," he muttered, resting his cheek on her hair.

Over his shoulder, Angie saw Darla and Gay exchange stunned, fascinated looks and then slip out with almost comic stealth. That quickly, she put them out of her mind, her full attention on the man holding her so carefully yet so very desperately.

"I'm all right, Rhys," she whispered, wanting only to ease the suffering in his beautiful gray eyes. Had she once thought his face hard to read? It seemed impossible now that she hadn't always seen the deep emotion simmering beneath the shuttered mask this extraordinary man had worn for so long.

"Are you in pain?" he demanded, sweeping a glance down the length of her sheet-covered body. And then he made a face and spoke before she had a chance to answer, "Of course you're in pain. Your poor legs."

"It's not too bad, Rhys," she assured him with shameless disregard for the truth.

His expression told her she couldn't fool him. "It's bad," he disputed flatly. "And your head hurts, doesn't it?"

She was too busy taking inventory of him to answer the obvious. There was a bandage on the back of his neck, another on his right cheek. Both forearms were bandaged and there were a few minor burns on his hands. If those had once been bandaged, he'd unwrapped them. "Are there any burns I can't see?" she asked him, trying to keep her voice steady.

"No. I'm okay. Don't worry about it."

She locked her eyes with his. "You saved my life, Rhys. I've never known anyone who's ever done anything as brave as what you did for me."

He flushed endearingly. "Don't, Angelique. I did what anyone would have done."

She smiled tremulously at his embarrassment, lifting her hand to his cheek. "Just your average, everyday type of hero, huh?"

He caught her hand in his and held it against his mouth, his eyes closing. His voice was raw when he spoke against her skin. "There was nothing heroic about it. I had to get you out of there. *I had to.* If you had died, I would have died with you. Don't you know that?"

Shaken to the core, her fingers trembled in his near-crushing trip. "Rhys—"

His eyes opened, and the sheen of moisture in them brought a wave of hot tears to her own. "I've been alone from the time I was three years old—hell, I've been alone all my life. I thought there was something wrong with me, some reason I didn't deserve to be loved or needed. Iris and Graham—well, they taught me a lot about caring, but they had their own lives, their own families. But you—you needed me. I told myself it was only for a little while, that you were young and self-sufficient and could have anyone or anything you wanted."

"I want you," she broke in, her voice constricted by the tightness of her throat.

"I know," he replied. "For some incomprehensible

reason, you want me. And I want you. I need you, Angelique. And I *will not* lose you," he added fiercely, spacing his words for emphasis.

He kissed her palm. "So you see," he continued more gently, "what I did wasn't heroic. It's probably one of the more selfish things I've ever done."

Heedless of the tears streaming down her bruised cheeks, she stroked his jaw with her fingertips. "I love you," she murmured.

"I love you, Angelique." He leaned over to kiss her again, then raised his head a few inches and gave her a slightly unsteady smile. "Saving your cat—now *that* was heroic," he mused, obviously feeling a need to lighten the mood.

She scowled at him. "You could have been killed going back into that house! That wasn't heroic, it was foolish! How could you risk your life for a cat?"

"It was your cat," he answered simply. "And, anyway, I knew where she was. She wasn't far inside."

She couldn't continue to scold him when she was so very grateful to him. The thought of her beloved pet dying so horribly made her shudder. "Oh, Rhys, thank you. I wouldn't have risked your life for anything, but I'm so glad she wasn't hurt."

He smiled and held up his hand to exhibit a long, angry-looking scratch. "Too bad the cat wasn't so grateful. She was scared and she was mad and she did *not* appreciate being pulled out of the hiding place she'd found under a chair. Ever heard a cat cough? She was coughing and cussing a blue streak all the way out of the house."

Angie cocked an eyebrow at him, then suppressed a grimace, knowing better than to let Rhys see that the slight gesture had set her head to throbbing again.

"Flower was cursing?" she repeated skeptically, rather surprised at his uncharacteristic whimsy.

He nodded gravely. "Fluently."

"Are you sure it wasn't you?"

"I did my share," he admitted. Finally releasing her hand, he spread the sheet more snugly over her and stood. "You look beat, sweetheart. Why don't you try to get some sleep?"

Knowing he was probably understating her appearance, she didn't bother arguing. "I think I will," she murmured, squirming slightly against the sheets in a vain attempt to get comfortable.

"I'm calling for some pain medication," he announced flatly when she couldn't hold back a slight moan. "It'll help you rest."

"No, Rhys, I don't—"

But he'd already pushed the button, giving her a look that dared her to argue with him. She sighed and gave up, knowing that the man her co-workers called the "dictator" was back in full swing. He was quite adept at hiding his gentle, vulnerable side when it suited his purposes.

He wouldn't be an easy man to live with, she reflected, her eyes closing. It would be a very long time, if ever, before he'd feel comfortable expressing his deepest feelings, though he'd proven that he could do so quite eloquently when inclined. And she loved him so much she ached with it, knowing she wouldn't change a thing about him even if she could.

He was Rhys. And he was hers. For always.

ANGIE MADE A FACE as she read the Sunday newspaper article early the next morning. One of the nurses had thought she'd want to see it and had brought her the paper with her breakfast. After a matter-of-fact description of the gas buildup that was being blamed for the explosion—pending further investigation—the story dealt in hyperbolic detail on the dramatic rescue by one of Birmingham's wealthiest and most prominent businessmen, lingering on the spicy hint that Rhys had been arriving at his fiancée's house at that late hour. The fiancée, it added, was the daughter of Nolan St. Clair, the Boston financier who'd been sentenced to prison earlier that year for tax evasion and other accounting mispractices.

After an extremely uncomfortable night, that wasn't exactly the way Angie would have chosen to start her day.

By midmorning the telephone on her bedside table began to ring. Gay, Darla, June and Kim each called to check on her and ask if she needed anything. Mickey insisted on talking to her to ascertain for himself that she was all right, earnestly promising that he'd take excellent care of Flower until Angie was out of the hospital.

Angie hung up for the fourth time chewing her lip thoughtfully. It seemed that everyone knew about her father by now. If it made any difference to the friends she'd made since arriving in Birmingham, she certainly couldn't tell. Had all her friends in Boston wanted to be with her only because of social reasons? Were her friends here in Birmingham truly less judgmental, more accepting—or was it she who had changed? Maybe, she reflected, she'd chosen her friends in Boston for all the wrong reasons. Maybe she'd been as guilty as they of making money and social-position requirements for entry into her exclusive circle. Maybe she'd given more of herself to these new friends, having had nothing else to offer them. It was certainly something to think about.

Staring sightlessly at her lap, she frowned as she considered the rather philosophical questions.

"What's wrong? Are you hurting? Do you need something for pain?"

Angie hadn't even realized Rhys had entered the room until he spoke from the side of the bed, his tone urgent. She looked at him in indulgent exasperation, noting that he seemed much better than he had when she'd finally convinced him to leave her bedside the night before. She wished she could say the same for herself. She must look terrible. "I'm not in pain, Rhys— well, not too much, anyway. I was just thinking."

He spotted the newspaper lying by her side and scowled. "Where'd you get that?"

"One of the nurses brought it to me."

"Which one?" he demanded, appearing ready to do battle.

"Rhys, it's all right. She thought I'd like to see it. And she was right."

"You didn't want to read that garbage," he refuted instantly.

"No," she admitted. "But I needed to know what was said. It's not as bad as it could have been. At least the article didn't mention all the questioning I was subjected to during my father's indictment."

"There was no need to mention your father at all," he stated with a moue of distaste toward the paper. "He had nothing to do with what happened to your house."

She made a dismissive gesture with her hand. "He's a very thorough reporter. Did his research to find out if there was anything interesting about the future wife of WakeTech's CEO. Found out there was. That's his job."

"His job is to report news, not gossip. The explosion was news. That stuff about your father was gossip."

"Did you come here to see me or to discuss journalism ethics?" she asked sternly, leveling him a mock-indignant glare.

He smiled and leaned over to kiss her. "To see you. How'd you sleep?"

"I've had more comfortable nights," she admitted. "And I missed you."

"I tried to stay. You threw me out."

"You needed some rest," she replied, then smiled. "And a shower."

He chuckled. "Point taken. I've had a couple of showers since I left here last night. One as soon as I got home, another this morning, after I'd spent a couple of hours looking over your place."

"You went by my house?"

He nodded, his smile fading. "Yeah. I wanted to see how much damage was done."

She swallowed. "Was anything left?"

His eyes gave her the answer even before he spoke. "I'm afraid not. The fire spread too quickly for the firefighters to bring it under control. They were lucky to prevent damage to your neighbors' homes."

She wouldn't cry, she told herself firmly, squaring her chin. After all, the important thing was that she and Rhys were safe and together. "I'm glad no one else was hurt," was all she said.

Somewhat awkwardly Rhys held out a paper bag he'd been clutching in one hand since he'd entered the room. "I did find this," he said quietly. "It was the only thing I spotted that hadn't sustained too much damage to be salvaged."

Hampered by having one arm still immobilized by the IV, she motioned for him to open the bag for her. He did, drawing out a silver rectangle and extending it solemnly toward her.

The glass was shattered, the silver blackened and dented, but by some miracle the photograph of her grandparents that had sat for so long on the delicate piecrust table was undamaged. Their lined, loving faces smiled up at her as she tired to focus through a mist of tears. "Oh, Rhys."

He groaned softly and sat beside her, stroking her head with one unsteady hand. "I'm sorry, Angelique. I know it's not much. All your things—"

She shook her head forcefully, the tears dislodged by the movement to trickle down her cheek. "No, you don't understand. I'm not disappointed. This is the one thing I would have saved if given the choice. Thank you, Rhys."

His thumb made a gentle swipe at one wet tear path. "I know most of your stuff was irreplaceable for sentimental purposes, but we'll contact your insurance company first thing tomorrow. Your friends have offered to do some shopping for you until you're on your feet, and you'll stay with me, of course. You don't have to worry about anything having to do with finances, you understand? I'll take care of you."

"I know you will, Rhys." She didn't point out that she was perfectly capable of taking care of herself— had, in fact, done so quite adequately when faced with similar circumstances earlier that year. Rhys needed to feel needed by her. Having felt exactly the same way about him, she understood. "And I don't want you feeling sorry for me, you hear? The legs will mend. I'll be back on my feet in no time. The doctor promised that there would be very little scarring, though I wasn't particularly worried about that."

"He probably assumed you would be. Most incredibly beautiful women tend to be a bit vain. You're the exception."

She caught his hand and kissed it. "You sweet talker, you." She knew exactly how she looked at the moment—bruised, battered, tangled and pale. Only someone who loved her could refer to her as an incredibly beautiful woman just then.

"What I'm trying to say, Rhys, is that I consider myself a very lucky person. When my world crashed down before, it left me with nothing—no family, no friends, no self-respect, very few possessions. I was devastated. This time I have no possessions left, except this—" she hugged the photograph to her chest "—and it doesn't matter. The friends I've made know about my father and don't seem to care at all, I've earned my own way long enough to know that I can continue to do so and, most importantly, I have you. How could I possibly complain?"

"I want you to marry me. Immediately. Now that the press is keeping an eye on us, I don't want them reporting that we're living together without benefit of marriage."

She chuckled. "Rhys, that's so old-fashioned. No one will care if we live together before the wedding."

"I care," he corrected her implacably, jaw squared. "I'm sorry if you were hoping for a big church wedding with all the trimmings—"

"I wasn't," she interrupted quickly.

"Good. Then we'll be married here, before you leave the hospital, as quickly as I can arrange it."

"Here?" she repeated weakly, looking around the hospital room. It was true that she hadn't envisioned a lavish church ceremony, but she hadn't really pictured a hospital room as her wedding chapel, either. Nor had she thought she'd be flat on her back in bed with two broken legs.

"Here." His tone brooked no argument.

Rhys would protect her from anything within his power, she thought ruefully—fire, engineers bearing deceptively innocent-looking drinks, gossip from people they'd never even met. She would have to talk to him about this tendency of his to be a bit overprotective. Later.

"All right," she agreed quietly. "If that's what you want." And then she smiled. "I'm really glad you'd already asked me to marry you before this happened. I'd hate to have you wondering if I was only marrying you for your money, now that I've nothing of my own."

His head lifted arrogantly. "If I'd thought you were the kind of woman who'd marry for money, I never would have asked you," he informed her with a trace of the steel-edged self-assurance that made him so intimidating to those who didn't know him as well as she did. And she believed him. Rhys wasn't a man who'd be fooled by anyone, including a woman he wanted.

He threaded her fingers through his, looking down at their linked hands to avoid her eyes. "I've never had a family, Angelique," he said with no trace of arrogance in his voice now. "I've always wanted one very badly. I promise I'll be a good husband to you, and a good father to our children, despite my lack of experience in either area."

"I know you will, darling," she assured him tenderly, her chest tightening almost painfully. His eyes shot up at the endearment, smoldering hotly as they met hers. "I love you."

"I have loved you from the moment you walked into my office," he told her, unfamiliar emotions making his words stiff. "You looked so cool and so self-confident, your chin stuck out as if daring me to reject you—and yet I could tell that you'd been hurt badly, that you were still hurting despite your brave attempt to hide your feelings behind a wall of icy professionalism."

His high, lean cheeks tinged with a touch of pink as he shifted restlessly on the bed beside her. Angie stared at that betraying color in fascination as he murmured, "You teased me about reading Yeats. Every time I looked at you during those first few months, when I wanted you so badly and thought I'd never have you, I kept remembering something he wrote."

"What?" Her question was only a breath of sound.

The color deepening in his face, he grimaced. "I've never been the type to quote poetry to a woman, but...'How many loved your moments of glad grace, and loved your beauty with love false or true, but one man loved the pilgrim soul in you, and loved the sorrows of your changing face.'"

She blinked back the tears she knew would make him even more uncomfortable. "That's lovely. Thank you." She managed a smile. "I have a quote from Yeats of my own that seems appropriate."

He lifted an eyebrow in question.

"'But I, being poor, have only my dreams; I have spread my dreams under your feet; Tread softly because you tread on my dreams.'"

"I love you." His voice was raw, deep, utterly sincere. She knew his wedding vows would be pledged no more or no less solemnly than those three words.

"I love you, Rhys."

Leaning over her, he gathered her tenderly into his arms, burying his face in her tangled hair. She snuggled willingly into the embrace, blinking back tears as she was touched again by the vulnerability of this very strong, very hard and once very much alone man. She vowed silently to herself and to him that he would never be alone again. Nor would she.

PERHAPS THERE'D BEEN a time when Angie had daydreamed of a huge church wedding. A white lace gown with a twenty-foot train, a bevy of attendants in organdy pastels, masses of roses and orchids, classical music played by an accomplished organist. She would have said then that she wanted that type of wedding. Now she knew that no wedding ceremony could ever be more beautiful than the one that made her Rhys's wife. Her bridal clothes a lacy white nightgown provided by her friends from work, her chapel a hospital room decorated with get-well bouquets of mums and carnations, a hospital chaplain officiating. Rhys wore one of his neat dark suits and a look of fierce satisfaction. The only witnesses were June and Graham, as Angie hadn't wanted to crowd the tiny room with guests.

Rhys slipped the heavy ring onto her finger with a long, intense look at her that made her throat tighten. And when he kissed her, his lips burned a brand on her that she knew would remain there for a lifetime. A possessive man, her husband, she thought in resignation. But one who'd willingly lay down his life for her. She had no complaints.

June tearfully congratulated them when the ceremony was over, hugging Angie and then tentatively offering a hug to her boss. He accepted it willingly.

And then Rhys turned to Graham, a touching smile softening his strong face. "I'd like to introduce you to my wife, Angelique," he said, as if he'd been practicing the words and couldn't wait to say them.

Smiling through a mist of tears, Angie watched in satisfaction as her husband's exuberant friend swept him into a hearty hug. "About damned time," Graham bellowed loudly enough to earn a shush from the hospital chaplain. "About damned time."

Rhys fervently agreed.

_____ Epilogue _____

MUTTERING IMPRECATIONS, Angie tossed the brass-topped cane into a corner as she entered the front door of the house she shared with her husband. She hated that cane.

Her bad mood dissipated immediately, as it almost always did, when she entered her living room, limping slightly as she walked. She'd turned Rhys's sparsely furnished, severely plain house into a real home in the fourteen months they'd been married. The furniture was comfortable, colorful, invitingly arranged. The walls were hung with beautiful oil paintings she and Rhys had chosen one by one. The glossy tables held the beginnings of a lifetime collection of mementos from special times in their young, happy marriage. A silver-framed photo of her grandparents sat on a piecrust table, almost a duplicate of her grandmother's. Rhys had found it for their first anniversary.

This was home, and she loved it. She loved everything in it. And yet she knew now that she could walk away from it all without a backward glance as long as Rhys walked at her side.

Flower entered the room with a welcoming meow, her mature black-and-white body sleek and graceful. Wincing in momentary envy of her pet's slender lines, Angie bent awkwardly to pat the affectionate cat. "You can look smug," she accused. "You won't ever be in this condition."

With a snort of complacent amusement, Flower turned and glided into another room. Angie straightened and rested a hand on her rounded stomach. She knew Rhys would be home soon. He'd been meeting all afternoon with a supplier in Montgomery. She knew he wouldn't stop by the office on his way home. Though as dedicated to his business as ever, Rhys had his priorities in much better order these days. Work was for working hours. Evenings were for family.

She hadn't been particularly surprised that he'd become fiercely protective in these first five months of her pregnancy—which explained her renewed use of the despised cane several months after she'd gleefully abandoned it. Because her ankle was still a bit unpredictable, Rhys was terrified that she'd fall and hurt herself or the baby. She'd given in to his urging to carry the cane only because she could tell he'd worry himself sick if she didn't.

She'd never forget the look on his face when she'd told him she was pregnant. She'd been trying ever since to precisely define the emotions she'd read in his eyes. Joy, apprehension, pride, anticipation, concern for her welfare. Perhaps even a touch of sheer terror at the thought of being a father at forty-two, after years of believing it would never happen. Angie had no such concerns. She thought Rhys would make a fantastic father. She even believed she'd make a pretty great mother. Together, the two of them could do anything.

"Angelique?" As always, Rhys called her name even before he'd closed the front door behind him.

"In here, Rhys." She turned with a smile to watch the doorway. Her smile deepened when he stepped through it, smiling back at her in that particularly sweet way he reserved only for her. The smile that always made her heart trip over itself.

He held up one paper-filled hand. "You forgot to get the mail. And you've thrown your cane in the corner again."

"I promised I'd use it outside the house. I refuse to use it in my own home."

He chuckled and crossed the room to kiss her. "I've accepted that compromise. Just stay close to a chair at all times."

"In case I feel like swooning when you smile at me?" she asked with mock innocence, her arms looping around his neck.

Grinning, he crossed his wrists behind her back. "Yeah, that's it."

"How was the meeting?"

"Dull. But productive. Did Henderson call?"

"Mmm-hmm. You really shook him up when you yelled at him last week. He was more organized and businesslike than he's ever been. He didn't even call me 'babe' this time."

"Good. Maybe I won't fire him after all."

Angie tugged his head down to kiss him again. "I missed you today," she murmured when she released his mouth.

His eyes lit with pleasure—and the faintest hint of surprise that always twisted her heart. It was still hard for Rhys to believe at times that there was someone who loved him so completely, who put him before everything else in her life. "Let's go out for dinner tonight," he suggested. "We can go to Rose's for Chinese, if you like."

Stepping back, Angie smoothed her maternity sweater over her skirt. "Sounds wonderful. You know

I can't resist Rose's twice-cooked pork. Oh, by the way, Graham called this afternoon."

Rhys looked up from the mail he was flipping through. "Did he want anything special?"

Angie laughed and shook her head. "Said he just wanted to see how I was doing. He swears he's already bought the baby a pony. You don't think he really has, do you?"

"I wouldn't put it past him. Let's hope he's teasing." He looked back down at the mail, then extracted one plain white envelope. "A letter from your father."

Angie reached for it. "I'll read it when we get back from dinner."

"And you'll answer it?" he asked just a bit too casually.

"Yes, Rhys," she replied patiently, "I'll answer it. Haven't I answered all his letters during the past year?" It had been Rhys who'd engineered the tentative reconciliation between Angie and Nolan, claiming that she would never be at peace until she'd resolved things with her father.

Nolan had been touchingly grateful to have the lines of communication open. It was the first time Angie could remember that she and her father had been completely honest with each other. There'd been a lot of hurts, years of emotional distance separating them, but she thought they could maintain an amicable relationship with a little compromise on each side. Nolan was particularly delighted with the news that he would have a grandchild soon.

"You know," Rhys said, his expression wary, "your father will be released next year."

"I know."

"He'll be needing a job—and it won't be easy to find one with his record."

She tensed. "Rhys—"

He held out a hand, palm outward. "Now listen before you automatically say no. I thought maybe I could offer him a job with WakeTech. Even you have to admit that he's good."

"You wouldn't be doing this if he wasn't my father."

"Probably not," he admitted. "That relationship may get him the job if he wants it, but it won't help him keep it. He'll have to prove that he can handle it and be of benefit to my company. Any screwing around and he's out on his butt. That will be made clear from the beginning. What do you think?"

"Rhys, are you sure? What will people say?"

He gave her The Look. "That doesn't concern me. As long as WakeTech's making money, no one has a right to say anything about how I choose to run it. Yours is the only opinion that matters. If it makes you uncomfortable, I won't offer."

Conceding to her husband's typical arrogance, Angie placed her father's letter on a table to be opened later. "I'll think about it," she promised. "In a way, I'd like to know that he'll have someplace to go, something to do that will keep him out of trouble. I just hope you know what you're doing."

"I always know what I'm doing," he replied, and this time his arrogance held a note of teasing.

"Yes, you do, don't you?" She lifted a hand to his face, her smile fading. "You're a very special man, Rhys Wakefield. I love you."

"If I'm special in any way," he returned huskily, "it's *because* you love me." He leaned over to kiss her, murmured, "I love you, Angelique," and then straightened and cleared his throat. "Do you want to change or are you ready to eat?"

She answered promptly. "I'm starving."

His loving smile taking her in from the top of her golden head to the tip of her toes, lingering lovingly on the precious bulge at her middle, Rhys slipped an arm around her shoulders and turned with her toward the door. "We can't have that. Let's go."

Angie cast one last, affectionate look at their home as Rhys escorted her out, a protective hand poised to steady her if she should stumble. She was one lucky woman, she thought contentedly, and it had nothing to do with money or social position. Rhys's love provided all the wealth she could ever desire.

American HEROES

AGAINST ALL ODDS

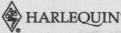

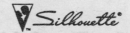

Please address questions and book requests to: Harlequin Reader Service U.S.: 3010 Walden Ave.,
P.O. Box 1325, Buffalo, NY 14269 CAN.: P.O. Box 609, Fort Erie, Ont. L2A 5X3   PAHGEN

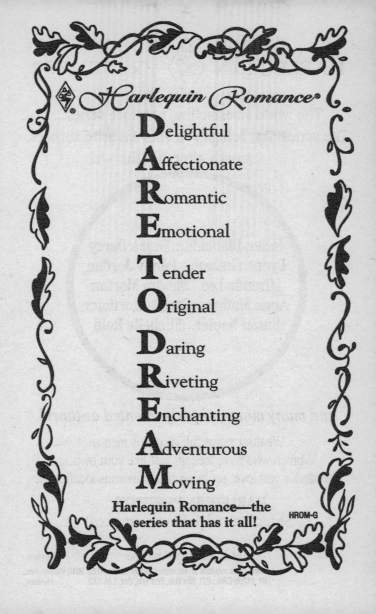

Harlequin Romance®

Delightful
Affectionate
Romantic
Emotional

Tender
Original

Daring
Riveting
Enchanting
Adventurous
Moving

**Harlequin Romance—the
series that has it all!**

HROM-G

HARLEQUIN ✦ PRESENTS®

The world's bestselling romance series...
The series that brings you your favorite authors,
month after month:

Helen Bianchin...Emma Darcy
Lynne Graham...Penny Jordan
Miranda Lee...Sandra Morton
Anne Mather...Carole Mortimer
Susan Napier...Michelle Reid

and many more uniquely talented authors!

Wealthy, powerful, gorgeous men...
Women who have feelings just like your own...
The stories you love, set in exotic, glamorous locations...

HARLEQUIN PRESENTS,
Seduction and passion guaranteed!

Harlequin® Historical

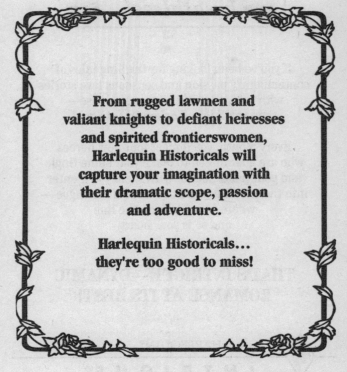

From rugged lawmen and
valiant knights to defiant heiresses
and spirited frontierswomen,
Harlequin Historicals will
capture your imagination with
their dramatic scope, passion
and adventure.

Harlequin Historicals...
they're too good to miss!

HHGENR

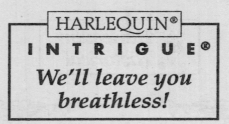